The Widower's Secret

A Sophie Quinn FBI Mystery Thriller

Book 3

Georgia Wagner

Publisher: Greenfield Press Ltd

Contents

Prologue

I'm not forgetting anything, Josephine told herself. She presented the thought as if it were evidence for the consideration of a jury, a task she'd grown exceedingly comfortable with over her decade of work as a prosecutor. No speculation. No hint of a question. Simple fact.

But that confidence did not solve the puzzle in front of her.

A glass of wine. Candlelight. Soft music. And if she wasn't mistaken, the enticing aroma of chicken dancing between fragrant notes of mushrooms, artichokes, and lemons.

Checking her cellphone again, Josephine confirmed it was 10:03 PM. When she'd pulled her Bentley to the front of the house, she'd assumed that the lights through the curtains of the bay windows were the telltale sign that Jonathan's work day had not yet come to an end. He often burned the midnight oil just as she did, staying at the trading office well after the markets closed and often sleeping at erratic intervals to make time for international calls. It was not at all unusual for Josephine to come home to her husband pacing the living room as he brokered some deal in French or Mandarin, his charming Gulf Coast drawl suppressed by practice and will.

But that didn't explain the candles, the wine, or the chicken.

An anniversary? No, she'd ruled that out first. Her calendar 55apps had not flagged her for any of those insipid Hallmark holidays, her husband's birthday, or any notable day that would demand some level of emotional attention from her. It wasn't her birthday either, she'd made sure to double-check her schedule for that as well.

So why did her home smell like rosewood candles and a romantic dinner for two?

Returning her cellphone to her bag, she hung the fine leather purse on a hook near the hallway table, beside the wine, and Josephine's lips pulled softly toward her left cheek. Not quite a smirk.

He had not come running to greet her at the door, not that he normally would. No, he was trusting her curiosity would pull her to the dining room without him needing to beg—without putting him in a place of having to do anything as demeaning as 'ask'. Her husband was nothing if not a shrewd negotiator. If there was no obvious explanation, then it must be something specific to her husband. Something he wants.

Removing her jacket, Josephine undid the top buttons of her blouse, adjusting her bra and tousling her dark brown hair in a way she knew drove Jonathan's 'caveman brain' wild. Then, checking herself once in the hallway mirror, she rolled up the hem of her pencil skirt. She still didn't know what this was, but if she was going into negotiations with her husband, she would not be going in 'unarmed'.

Giving her lips a small bite to put some color in them, Josephine lifted the wine glass and took a luxuriant drink. Red, rich, and with a slight oaky note that she couldn't place. It reminded her of one of Jonathan's favorites... yes, it was nearly identical if not for that dark, woody undertone. She carried the glass with her as she followed the flicker of candlelight into the dining room.

As she crossed the threshold, Josephine felt the small, invisible hairs of her arm stand on end. The tactical thoughts about what she would say and how she would say it vanished, drowned beneath an inarticulate feeling like the tension before a lightning strike.

All at once, the lights in the house died, leaving only the orange flicker of the candles in the adjacent room. And as she crossed the entry hall and rounded the ornately carved open doorway to the dining room, Josephine found she was holding her breath.

Jonathan sat at the head of their polished dining room table, an elaborate piece of Turkish Olive Wood. The banquet she'd smelled was spread from end to end and filled all between with candles. Her husband looked up to her, his eyes wide.

A black gag was tied between his teeth, and a red run of blood glimmered wetly across his forehead. Josephine screamed, her hand instinctively going to her mouth, the half-empty wine glass falling from her shocked fingers and shattering on the hardwood floor. Jonathan made a muffled grunting noise, like someone shouting into a pillow. He shook in his chair, his wrists tied to the arm rests.

Josephine turned. She had to get her phone. To call the police.

With one hand on the doorframe, she froze.

A white face hovered in the darkness, bobbing softly, like a ghost's severed head. Eyes as black as a hollow skull, overwrought cheeks turned down in a sobbing frown under a pinched brow, the whole aspect frozen in this silent tableau of pain and sorrow.

A mask.

Josephine's terrified mind pulled the word from the blackness as a shadowy silhouette stepped out from the now pitch-dark entry hall. The figure was clad from boots to throat in black, all except for the porcelain white of the weeping mask.

With a scream, Josephine grabbed a bowl of couscous from the table and threw it at the figure.

The mask's arms came up defensively, blocking the bowl and speckling its sleeves in yellow grains and finely minced vegetables. Josephine took her chance. Ducking under the raised arms, she bolted for the front door.

She had to get her phone. She had to get out. A loud, insistent part of her knew that she and Jonathan were dead if she didn't.

Josephine had nearly crossed the threshold when a gloved hand caught her around the waist. She reflexively threw an elbow, feeling a solid *thunk* as it struck the mask's hip. Half-remembered courses in self-defense, not practiced in more than a decade, were coming back in snap shots, and Josephine lifted her heel to stomp on the attacker's foot.

But with one foot in the air, she was off balance. And with a shove, the mask tossed her back against the dining room table. The candlelight flared wildly and one long candle stem fell beside her into the mashed potatoes, quenched with a hiss.

The masked figure raised a dark hand and pointed to one of the table's vacant seats, slowly, condemningly, like the Ghost of Christmas Future showing Scrooge his own gravestone. Josephine flinched, but after the barest second, she darted to the far side of the room.

The kitchen door.

She could cut through the kitchen and escape through the back. She could get out—get to a neighbor—

Her hip struck the kitchen counter, and Josephine spun. She felt unsteady on her feet as if the whole house were the deck of a ship rolling under her. Throwing both hands to the counter, she held on for dear life, trying to steady her feet.

The room swam around her, and suddenly she felt exhaustion tugging at her eyelids.

Yes, she could feel it now, in her legs, in her arms.

Numbness.

The wine, she thought briefly. Her husband wasn't the one who left it for her...

The mask hovered into the kitchen, patiently meandering toward her. No sign of hurry in its steps at all.

Josephine let out a pitiful groan, shoving off the counter with the little control she had left over her muscles. She fell, in tumbling steps, to the glass door of the back porch. A hundred yards of carefully manicured grass. A hedge. And the distant lights of her nearest neighbor's back patio. She saw smoke, and a distant part of her wondered if the Browns were having a late-night barbeque.

Pawing at the latch, she couldn't feel anything now. It was as if her whole body had been put under anesthesia.

"Please," Josephine murmured, but the sound was thick and formless as the drugs in her system robbed her of even the ability to beg for her life.

The mask put a hand on her shoulder, the other under her arm. And step by step, Josephine felt herself led back to the dining room. To sit across from her husband, tears streamed down his face now as Josephine looked down at ropes that she could not feel binding her to her seat.

Chapter 1

There had to be a way to make the numbers work.

Sophie idly chewed her lip, sighing through her nose and shifting in the uncomfortable, creaking hospital room chair as she stared at a hole through her laptop's screen. The chill of the air conditioning left a dewy mist on the edges of the window into the early morning bake of a Louisiana summer.

She tried to ignore the beep of the heartrate monitor, the distant clack of heels on tile hallways, and the muted coughing from other rooms. And with all the focus she could muster, she tried not to look at the bed, set against the far wall, just beside the gently flashing screen emitting that steady, digital chime.

She had lined up three separate windows on her computer to compare them side by side. The first was her own bank account, commitments and payment history stacked to give her the scope of her personal finances; the last reserves of what Sophie Quinn had plundered from her assets six years ago when she'd given up a thriving career as a globe-trotting magician, mentalist, and hypnotist to hunt the madman who had murdered her sister... the man who had nearly murdered her. It was not an insignificant sum... but private investigators, bribes, and buying the tools to fuel her personal crusade against the River Killer had made the end of that money a question of *when* rather than *if*.

Clicking to the second window, she reviewed the latest bill from the Baton Rouge hospital she currently sat in. Noah and Zadie Quinn had never put much stock in insurance. There was a good deal of smiling and talk of 'relying on the Lord to provide', but from the moment Sophie was old enough to understand what health insurance was, she had quietly assumed it had more to do with the family's flirtatious relationship with poverty and Noah's gravitational pull towards work that paid 'under the table' than with Zadie Quinn's spiritual convictions.

The man in the hospital bed stirred. A twitch really, just enough to let a quiet rustle out from the blankets. Sophie's gaze leapt to him. But her father, Noah, had gone still again, the heartrate monitor keeping its chipper, metronome beat as steady as it had been before.

She rubbed her eyes, then feeling tension in her spine, Sophie rolled her neck and let her close-cropped, auburn hair briefly touch against the slate grey of her suit coat's shoulder. She'd been in this hospital on and off for nearly a week now, ever since her mother had called in a panic to tell her that her father had been shot. They slept in shifts, Sophie watching him while Zadie was at home resting and gathering tupperware dinners from the well-meaning members of her church.

When her father hadn't woken up after the first two days, Sophie started to prepare herself for the worst. But her father held on. His heavy keg of a chest, caught between old muscle and a more recent beer belly, continued to rise and fall. His heart beat. And when he lay flat on his back, he could saw wood as well as Sophie's childhood memories claimed. Once or twice nurses had even come by to ask if they could close the door against his incomparable snoring.

Returning her attention to her laptop, Sophie looked at the hospital bill once more... without insurance, the costs were astronomical... mounting every day that her father lay comatose. Sophie looked again at her own bank account, her eyes distant for a moment.

...and then she looked at the final window.

An encrypted chat program, run through a private network on a dark net browser. A window to a man who may be the missing link between Sophie and her quarry... between her vengeance and the River Killer.

Merchant's USB drive had provided the key, allowing Sophie to enter the anonymous chat site. Her mentor and the supervising agent for her current work with the Louisiana field office, Lidya Merchant had made it abundantly clear that if Sophie pursued the Mississippi Line Minutemen, the off-grid militia group that may have spawned RK's violent spree, Sophie could expect no further help from her or the FBI... she was on her own.

But Sophie was used to being on her own. She'd been on her own for six years before now, and she'd do it alone for sixty more if she had to.

Sophie scanned the chat log, the tense back and forth as the anonymous militia member negotiated with her, teasing out what she wanted... and what she was willing to pay to get it. An offer... a counter-offer... and there, at the very end of the log, the militia member's final offer, bookended with a terse 'Take it or leave it. I don't hang my ass out for chicken feed.'

Her father's hospital bills.

The militiaman's bribe.

Looking back to her account screen again, Sophie blinked. Somehow, somehow the numbers *had* to work...

"Morning, Sophie." The faint, cheerless words came from Sophie's mother as the large woman swept her way into the room like a wave arriving on the beach. Zadie didn't look at her daughter, instead making a bee-line for her husband, her flats squeaking on the polished tile.

Sophie murmured back a soft good morning of her own as Zadie leaned down and planted a tender kiss on her unconscious husband's forehead, stroking his thin hair and wiping away the mark her kiss had left in the same motion. Her eyes were ringed with red, exhaustion and tears both leaving their signs. Her bright, floral clothing was as immaculate as ever, but Sophie noticed the small creases and wrinkles at the seams... a signal as clear to her as a plaque painted with the words: I'm not alright.

"He hasn't woke up yet?" Zadie asked, interrupting Sophie's thoughts.

Sophie shook her head, then, as her mother hadn't looked her way yet, she said, "No. The doctors are still saying the same thing. The gunshot is healing well, but the head trauma he took when he fell is still complicating things."

"But you're watchin' him, right? You're not just goin' by what the nurses and doctors are telling you? You stay with him when I'm not here, right?" Zadie cast an accusing glare at the laptop open in Sophie's lap.

"Yes, Mama," Sophie replied, her cheeks flushing as her own exhaustion and frustration crept into her answer. "I haven't gone anywhere."

"Don't get sharp with me, child. Not today." Shaking her soft chin, Zadie touched a finger to the corners of her eyes and crossed to find her usual place on the small, hard sofa the hospital kept for visitors.

Sophie's mouth drew into a thin-lined approximation of a smile, and she took a steadying breath. She had to keep the peace. She and her mother had their differences, but things were tense enough before her father was shot.

"I don't understand how you can keep working at a time like this," Zadie continued. "With your daddy in the state he's in. I swear to God, Sophie, sometimes I don't know what to make of you."

Sophie tried to hold her tongue. She took another breath. It's ok. She's just upset. Her husband is in the hospital and...

"I remember when you used to laugh and smile all the time," Zadie continued. She didn't look at Sophie, instead fiddling with the sunflower zipper of her purse in her lap as she spoke. "Couldn't keep a grinnin' off that face of yours. Now I look at you sometimes, and you got this... this cold look to your eyes. Dark eyes, like-a gator's eyes."

Sophie's jaw clenched. She kept her eyes on the laptop screen. But as Zadie opened her mouth again, her daughter cut her off. "The world doesn't stop turning, Mama. Not for you, not for me. Not for anyone. The doctors are doing everything they can—"

"I'm not talkin' about the doctors, Sophie. I'm talking about *you*, and—"

"And I'm doing what you asked me. I'm sitting. Watching. I'm here, aren't I?"

"Are you?" Zadie asked, her voice brittle, her eyes glossing with ready tears.

Sophie gripped her laptop like a lifeline, the plastic letting out soft ticks of protest at the pressure. "I tried to get you out of that trailer park *years* ago. I could have bought you a house anywhere in the country. He didn't have to be there."

"Doesn't matter who our neighbors could have been, Sophie. Your daddy is the same man in any state. When he sees trouble, he *helps*. That's who he is."

"Well, his good Samaritan act put him here and now we're the ones who have to pay for it."

"What are you saying? That he should've let those two men kill each other right outside our front door? I know we raised you better than that."

"It wasn't his fight. He didn't stop anyone from getting shot; he just made sure it was *him* that ended up on the other end of that gun. Fell over and cracked his head and now who knows even *if* he'll wake up—"

"Don't you say that!" Zadie interrupted, her voice trembling. "Don't you *dare* say that about your own flesh and blood, Sophie Quinn."

Sophie wanted to stop. A small voice in her warned her. But the dam had burst, and six years of resentment flowed through her the way an old wound throbs under storm clouds. Turning to meet her mother's eyes, she lowered her voice. "I could have moved you out of Peillon seven years ago. I could have taken you away while Molly was still alive—while we were all still safe. That place," Sophie felt her lungs shudder as she took another breath, the cold feeling in her limbs no longer just from the air vent above her. "One at a time, that place is going to eat everyone I love."

For a long moment, Zadie's mouth hung open. Like a landed fish, she stared, gaping, her eyes so watery that a passing nurse might have believed she'd just been slapped. Sophie's stomach fell. Her own lips hung open and she idly licked at them, blinking as she slowly fought to unclench the fingers driving her own nails into her palms like self-inflicted stigmata.

At that moment, Sophie's cell phone began to vibrate in her pocket. Once. Twice. Then, without breaking eye contact with her mother, Sophie raised the phone to her ear.

"Quinn," she said softly.

"Miss Quinn, it's Agent Greer." A polite masculine voice, confident and full, with a slight sandpaper edge that hinted at the restrained capacity for commanding shouts or perhaps a long-dead cigarette habit. A voice that Sophie couldn't help but feel an odd sense of comfort in. Though, she supposed, having your life saved once or twice will do that. "We have a body," Greer continued, "a second body, I should say. Merchant asked me to reach out to see if you'll come in on this one. I know your family needs you, so I understand if you can't—"

"Text me the address," Sophie interjected.

Hanging up her phone, she looked down at her laptop, glancing between the three open screens. Her informant's demanded payout. Her father's hospital bills... Her own rapidly dwindling funds. "I'm sorry, Mama—"

Zadie held up a hand, shaking her head. "Just go," she said, looking to her husband's hospital bed. "Like you said, 'the world doesn't stop turning'. Not for Sophie Quinn."

Chapter 2

Arsonists. Vandals. And murderers.

When Sophie had plunged herself into her criminology degree, she had been surprised to hear there was some truth to the old expression 'the criminal always returns to the scene of the crime'. Not a guarantee. There was no such thing in an investigation. But there was something primitively natural to a person's desire to see the results of what they had done, to stand back when the sculpture is finished and to see what it is that their own hands have made, even days later. To return to the scene.

Arsonists were some of the most common, watching from a distance as the fire they set spread, returning afterward to see the charred remains they created with a simple spark. Vandals frequently come back as well, sitting back as they voyeuristically enjoy the stooped custodian sweeping up glass from a window they shattered; seeing the shocked or admiring faces of passers-by as they take in the graffiti tagged up and down the bus stops and subway terminals.

But with murderers, they aren't looking at broken glass and burned out buildings. They're looking at the ruins of a life. A bleeding hole in a home or a community that they dug out with their own hands.

As Sophie pulled into Starlight Park gated community, she glanced through the light mist of a morning drizzle and scanned the shocked faces of the neighbors staring out from their windows or gathered on porches—respectfully distant from the police cruisers barring off the long driveway. She wondered if the killer was among them; if one of these alarmed faces could be a mask hiding a murderer's secret delight.

A trim, athletic woman in her fifties leaned against a car hood, staring at Sophie through a pair of dark sunglasses as if she'd been tracking her approach since the gate. Her silver hair was tied into a compact bun, and her black suit and matching umbrella would have been a perfect fit for a funeral.

"Ma'am," Sophie said by way of greeting as she parked in front of the woman, Supervising Agent Lidya Merchant, Sophie's oldest friend in the Bureau and in many ways, her mentor.

Merchant gave her a quick nod, glancing up and down the street as she stepped close enough for the pair to share her umbrella. Sophie wondered if the older agent had the same thoughts she'd had about the murderer returning to the scene. If she did, she kept them to herself.

Sophie turned toward the house but stopped when Merchant didn't take the first step to follow her.

"A moment, Quinn," Merchant said brusquely. "Meyers has been on my case about you. He wants to know when you're coming back to the Detroit field office, and I'm running out of excuses."

Nodding, Sophie looked out into the rain-damp neighborhood. "I'm not ready to go back yet," she said simply.

"I know. But the reasons I'm giving are starting to wear thin. People are asking questions about Sophie Quinn, about why I still need you down here for every odd case."

"Something I need to know?" Sophie asked tentatively. For a moment she thought of the secret USB Merchant had given her, and she wondered if the cunning older woman had been found out. It wasn't exactly FBI policy to hand out classified information for personal vendettas, after all.

"Nothing so far," Merchant murmured grimly. "But Meyers is starting to go over my head. He's left a couple messages with Hitchens."

At the mention of the pompous Deputy Director, Sophie scoffed, folding her arms and shaking her head. She could still remember the bloated, older man's coffee breath as he mocked her during the last case's briefing. In the end, she'd embarrassed him in front of his office and solved the case... though he was quick to claim as much credit as he could for bringing down the Coffin Killer.

"Let me guess, now Hitchens is on your back to get me out of Louisiana?"

"Bingo," Merchant replied.

"I can't just go back," Sophie said. "You know what I'm on to. It's the best lead I've had in years. Besides, my father's still in the hospital."

Merchant let out a sigh. "Right now, you have that excuse. But what about after?" Turning to fully face her, Merchant removed her sunglasses, her honey-brown eyes locking onto Sophie's. "Soon, you're going to have to make a choice. You're going to have to decide what you want."

Sophie felt her chest tighten. She wanted to find RK... she wanted to chase whatever leads she had until the man who tortured her and murdered her sister was in a cell or in the ground... She could tell Meyers and Hitchens and every FBI director from here to California to go hang, but then where would she be? Like it or not, she still needed their resources. PI's like Fabian St. Claire, the man who'd put her back on RK's track, they could only get her so much... She'd spent years floundering on her own, and it was her FBI connections that had given her a fighting chance.

Going back to Detroit would be the safe choice. Meyer liked her. He played by the book, but she wouldn't be in constant danger of losing her job... of losing those resources—Sophie thought again of her rapidly diminishing bank balance. Down here, though, Hitchens would keep looking for any reason to get her gone, to arrest her even. It wasn't safe, but she'd have allies... Merchant... Greer.

Merchant rolled her shoulders, adjusting the umbrella and sprinkling the ground around them with a wave of rain drops. "I don't need an answer now," she said. "But I need one soon. I can make you a full-time consultant down here. But I can't do it while you have a Detroit zip code. If you don't make the call, tell Meyer you're done in Detroit and make the move down here official," Merchant returned her sunglasses to her face, "this is your last case in Louisiana."

With the threat of those final words hanging in the air, Merchant strode toward the crime scene. For a moment, stunned by the abrupt finality of the statement, Sophie stood alone, the drizzle overhead slicking her short hair to her scalp and speckling her suit, then she hustled forward, following her mentor to the house in silence.

On the street, between two police cruisers and a white forensics van, Sophie recognized a white, four-door Interceptor, a 2017 Taurus her photographic memory reminded her. Greer must already be inside, she thought, and sure enough, as she crossed the threshold, among the black and brown uniforms of local police and FBI field techs stood the tall ex-Marine.

Jonathan Greer's tan suit had a warm look like the inside of a toasted almond, and as he turned to face her, his clear blue eyes meeting hers with a small crinkle of a smile at the edges, Sophie couldn't help but grin. Comfortable excitement fluttered in her stomach at the prospect of working alongside the coarsely handsome agent once again.

"Miss Quinn. Ma'am," Greer gave a respectful nod to Merchant before turning back to Sophie, "It's good to see you again. I've been meaning to visit, but—How's your father?"

Sophie blinked as she felt a pang of guilt tighten in her stomach. She gave a tense smile and waved away the question. "It's fine, really. He's still stable. We won't know how bad the head trauma is until he wakes up."

Greer gave her a solemn, sympathetic look. Sophie reflexively clocked the tug at his cheeks, his eyes, the centimeter-thin shift in his posture, all the check boxes her mentalism training looked for in genuine sympathy and worry. For a fraction of a second, the six-two, former Marine engineer looked every one of his forty years. At that moment, he seemed as if he might say more, but Merchant cleared her throat and the pair followed her gesture to an adjoining hallway.

"I have to check on a few things. Agent Greer, will you walk Miss Quinn through the crime scene?" Without waiting for an answer, Lidya Merchant retreated to another part of the house, her cell phone going to her ear as she did.

The home was one of the nicest Sophie had been in over the last several years. New hardwood—with no sign of warping or misalignment—met her athletic shoes as she followed Greer through the entry hall. A long, richly-carpeted stair swept to a second floor, drawing the eye to a glittering chandelier overhead, and an eclectic collection of modern paintings and decorative carvings filled the walls and doorways without cluttering them.

"The homeowners were a real power couple," Greer said. "The husband in finance, the wife a partner at a law firm. Their housekeeper discovered the scene when she came in this morning."

Stepping aside, Sophie saw a spilled bowl of what looked like yellow rice and vegetables. No, as she reached it, she could see now it was couscous. The spilled granules started from an adjacent room and spread into the hallway.

Greer ignored it though, stepping around the mess and the tiny, yellow flag marking it as evidence as he motioned through an entryway into the adjoining room. It was a spacious dining room, a long table surrounded by eight chairs filling the extravagant space.

The smell of room-temperature food was what hit Sophie first. Cold grease. The sour scent of wine left uncorked. A few flies buzzed in the otherwise silent room, hopping between shriveled strawberries and an herb-encrusted chicken that looked as if it were covered in stale sweat.

At the foot of the table was a curtained bay window that faced the home's front yard. A small bench was set with cubbies and filled with what seemed to be decorative, leatherbound books, *Treasure Island* and *Don Quixote* among others, their titles written in gilded lettering on spines that looked as if they'd never been cracked.

Between the feast and the book-filled bay window, at the foot of the table, sat the body of a woman in a fashionable business skirt and blouse. Her brown hair trailed over the back of the chair; her head lolled back to expose a fatal slash across her throat.

The other chairs all sat empty.

"Josephine Ramsey. Husband, Jonathan Sharpe. Watch your step," Greer said, stepping into the room. He pointed to the floor and a red stain glittering with bits of broken glassware, also marked with a small, yellow evidence flag. "Judging by the state of things, forensics is guessing dinner was served late last night. After eight PM at the earliest."

"Where's the husband?" Sophie asked, following Greer into the room.

"We don't know. We contacted his employer and he hasn't come into the office. There's no activity on his credit card. We're trying to see if we can get the home's security footage, but apparently, there was some sort of system failure. When we arrived, several fuses had been turned off."

"Blown out?" Sophie asked, raising an eyebrow.

"No, manually turned off. Someone killed the power to most of the home." Greer scratched at his scalp. "We're thinking the scene was by candlelight. You can see the wax burned all the way down. Whatever happened, whoever was here, they just let the candles burn as they left."

"Someone threw a bowl of food at another person," Sophie said softly, gesturing to the overturned bowl spilling into the hall.

Greer paused, looking down at the mess. "Someone definitely threw a bowl of... rice?"

"Couscous," Sophie corrected, but at Greer's questioning looks, she said, "It's not important."

"Fair enough. How do you know it was thrown *at* someone, though?"

Crouching down, Sophie drew the shape of the spilled food with her finger. "Look at how it's curved. One bowl but two arcs of mess on the ground, like a crescent moon."

Greer knelt beside her, following her finger as she pointed to the spilled couscous. "Probably the killer," he said in a low voice. "People will grab at anything to defend themselves when they're panicked. Do you think she threw the wine at him as well?"

"No." Sophie gingerly chewed her lip. "The heavier fragments of the glass are mostly together. The splatter of the wine looks like it was dropped too. If I had to speculate, I'd say she dropped the wine because she was scared, then tried to fight back with the bowl. I would bet you'll find Ms. Ramsey's prints on both."

Greer gave a low grunt of affirmation. "Not going to bet against you there. We'll get forensics to confirm."

Sophie looked back at the body. Victims of violent crime sometimes die with their fear written on their faces, freezing in those last moments of terror. But Josephine Ramsey looked... placid... almost peaceful. Sophie looked around the room. She attempted to piece the scene together, trying to imagine how the victim went from panicked and fighting to sitting docilely while someone cut her throat. "Do we have the murder weapon?" Sophie asked.

Shaking his head, Greer clicked his tongue. "No. We figure it's a kitchen knife, though. One is missing from the block in the next room."

Standing, Sophie paced the floor around the table. "Has anyone collected a sample of the wine yet?" Greer looked to the bottle on the table, but Sophie quickly rounded to the evidence flag on the floor. "No, the spilled wine."

"Not yet," Greer said waving over one of the nearby forensics techs and giving him quick directions as they spoke. "You're thinking she was drugged?"

"It would explain why she calmly sat and let her throat be cut," Sophie said. "Why her expression is so calm. The food may be drugged too, but nothing looks eaten."

Nodding in agreement, Greer said, "We'll know more when the coroner runs a tox screen. If she was roofied or anything like that, we'll find out."

Sophie turned a slow circle, looking around the room. She lifted a finger to her lips and gave it a light, puzzled bite as she did. A missing husband. A dead wife. A wealthy couple and what looked like a romantic dinner gone wrong. "I don't get it," Sophie said at last.

Greer shrugged. "Until we find otherwise, I think it's likely the husband."

"No," Sophie quickly added, shaking her head. "I mean, why am I here?"

The tall agent seemed taken aback, so Sophie elaborated. "The circumstances are odd and—" Sophie swept a hand towards the table, "—perhaps a little dramatic. But this feels like an ordinary murder investigation. And, as you said, it's likely the husband did it. Why did Merchant call me in on this?"

Realization abruptly spread on Greer's face, his mouth opening briefly then closing as he put his hand on his hip. "Merchant didn't tell you."

"Tell me what?" Sophie said.

"This is the second killing."

"What?" Sophie asked, spinning to directly face her partner.

"Another woman was killed less than ten miles from here, a small town called Coving Bridge. About five days ago. Same set up. Elaborate dinner. Romantic candles. Missing husband. Found the next morning with her throat cut at the dinner table."

Identical MOs... Sophie's brow beetled in concentration. "Have they found the husband yet?" she asked, her mind swiftly sorting through this new detail.

Greer's eyebrows briefly raised in confused resignation as he replied, "Yes. He walked into the local precinct the day after. Confessed to the killing and let himself be locked up. He hasn't given any *reasons*. Only insisting over and over that he'd murdered her."

Sophie's mind was reeling. "Any priors? History of violence?"

"Against his wife?" Greer shook his head. "No. There's a police report of him beating up a guy outside a nightclub a few weeks back but no arrest record. I'll send you the file."

"No charges after assaulting someone in public? That's bizarre."

"You're telling me," Greer grunted in agreement. That second, his cellphone lit up. "It's the local PD," he quickly explained as he answered. And after only a moment, he turned to face Sophie, his eyes narrowed in focus. "Sharpe? Yes. The victim's husband... A confession?"

Sophie closed her eyes, a cold dread settling into her chest. One killing like this was an oddity... But two?

No, where one was a coincidence, two was a conspiracy.

Chapter 3

"Is he lying?"

Greer looked down, glancing at Sophie out of the corner of his eyes. In answer to his question, her lips drew into a thin line.

Once again, the tall agent was reminded how he sometimes had trouble interpreting the younger woman's expressions. She had a way of controlling her features when she wanted to, making those commanding, hazel eyes as uncompromising as mirrors. Even when she smiled, it was hard for him to know what was going on in her mind. Maybe it was because she smiled so rarely? He didn't know yet, but he wondered if it had to do with being on a stage, learning to smile without really meaning it. Despite how close they had become, to Jonathan Greer, Sophie Quinn was still, in many ways, a mystery.

But in that moment, Greer had no trouble reading his new partner.

Confusion and frustration were the order of the day.

She glared through the one-way glass into the interrogation room where Mr. Jonathan Sharpe, Josephine Ramsey's husband, her *confessed* murderer, sat cuffed to a metal table in a set of business clothes that were rumpled in that particular way clothes do when someone has slept in them. With tears in his eyes, he called out again, shouting into the empty room.

"I did it. I killed her! I cut her throat with a kitchen knife. Please! I need to confess!" After another few overtures, the man's words dissolved into a fresh wave of sobs as his face hit his folded forearms.

"Do you want my honest opinion?" Sophie said at last.

Frankly, he thought the question unnecessary since everything he knew about Sophie Quinn told him she would be giving her unfiltered opinion regardless. But then again, manners make the man.

"Please," Greer said tapping the case file's plain manila exterior across his palm. They'd both taken a few minutes to review it, and while he had an excellent memory, he knew Sophie's eidetic mind could already read it back to him in full if he asked her to.

"He's lying," Sophie said plainly. "Too insistent. Too desperate."

"Sometimes killers feel remorse. They go too far and now they can't take it back," Greer said slowly.

But Sophie was already shaking her head. "No, there's grief there. Pain. He's not forcing that. But look at how he's repeating himself. Insisting even when no one's in the room. He's afraid we won't believe him. Why wouldn't we? The evidence points to him, and there's no other obvious suspect. Yet, he's terrified we won't convict him. And I can't, for the life of me, figure out why."

Greer was surprised to find that this answer didn't shock him. He'd been uneasy since Sophie had pointed out the victim's placid face at the crime scene. He hadn't been on site for the first murder, so he was coming at it with fresh eyes as well.

Still, the easy answer would be the husband.

Logically, they should take this confession as the easy win it should be. But something held him back. But where he had a bad feeling and instinct telling him something wasn't right, Sophie was able to give a name to it.

It was like she could see things in people, like all their secrets were an open book for her to read. Even secrets they were keeping from themselves. Greer remembered the way Sophie had spotted the secret his daughter Kinsley had been holding during their last case, a glimpse of the Coffin Killer that not even her own mind would let her remember. But Sophie had found it, and like a surgeon, she'd worked patiently to bring that memory to light.

If she said Mr. Sharpe was lying, he believed her.

"Why," Sophie repeated quietly. "Why are you lying?"

"Let's go find out," Greer said, his own voice low in his throat.

The first minute of their entrance was flooded by Jonathan Sharpe's animated confessions. Even with the dark rings under his eyes, the disheveled appearance of his clothing, and the uneven stubble breaking out over his face, Mr. Sharpe was the type of strong-jawed, broad-shouldered man that Greer had heard called 'classically handsome'. His body was evenly muscled in a way that told Greer he likely had a personal trainer. Definitely strong enough to overpower a woman like his wife and cut her throat with a kitchen knife, particularly if she was drugged.

When Sharpe's ravings began to subside, Greer held up a hand, pushing him the rest of the way to silence. It was all the same that they'd heard a dozen times over anyway.

"Mr. Sharpe," Greer began. "First of all, thank you for talking with us. You did the right thing coming in."

"I had to," Sharpe interjected. "I killed her. But I can't run. I can't live with myself after... after that."

"Yes," Greer said. "You've made that clear. But we had a few additional questions, we're hoping you can—"

"What other questions could you possibly have?" Sharpe exploded. His eyes shot wide, his hands slammed against the table with an abrupt clap. "Did you do it? Yes, I did. There! The only question that matters, and I *have* answered it. Bring me some paper. I'll sign a confession right now."

"Mr. Sharpe, please." Compared to the man's outburst, Sophie's voice was like a whisper. Cool and calm, subconsciously bringing the conversation back to level. Greer sat back, letting her talk.

"We want what you want. Everything must be air-tight. Set and squared. Right?"

Sharpe blinked once, twice, then swallowed hard and nodded back. Greer couldn't help but shake his head in admiration. How does she always manage to do that?

"Good. Thank you for helping us to close this case so quickly," Sophie continued. "We have a pretty clear idea of the night Josephine was murdered." Sophie glanced Greer's way and he gave a subtle nod. He'd seen it too. Sharpe had winced at the mention of his wife's name. "But we're having a harder time piecing together the night you killed Maya Rossi."

Maya was the first victim, the woman killed in Coving Bridge five days before. Her husband James had turned himself in four days ago, just like Sharpe was doing now. If there was a connection—a conspiracy between these murders—then Sharpe should know that.

Jonathan Sharpe froze, and Greer could see the cold sweat breaking out over the man's furrowed forehead in real-time. The suspect licked his lips, looking down at the table, his pupils flicking back and forth between his two hands, clutched together in front of him as if in prayer.

"...Maya R-Rosie?" He spoke with a heavy focus, like someone learning a new language and trying to find the pronunciation.

"Mrs. Rossi, the woman killed five days ago," Sophie prompted.

Sharpe looked as though he may burst into tears, concern and focus at war on his face as he clenched his jaw and began to violently shake his head. A sort of hissing sound leaked between his teeth that then exploded into a stuttered "Y-yes-ss... yes. Maya Rossi." He didn't look up, didn't meet either of their eyes as he swiftly added, "I killed her too. Five days ago."

Greer frowned. No new details. No elaboration. He was simply grasping at the same information Sophie and he had given him. Glancing to his partner, Greer caught a subtle shift of her chin. Lying.

Without a word, Greer watched Sophie reach into the inner pocket of her suit coat. A familiar brass pocketwatch emerged, and as she set it softly in front of her, Greer found his neck and shoulders tensing.

Hypnosis.

His daughter, Kinsley, had been a fan of Sophie's stage magic for years before they met. While she was away for the summer working as a camp counselor, Greer had borrowed a couple DVDs from his daughter's room. It was striking to see Sophie in her element. Her hair had been long back then, reaching past her shoulders in rich auburn waves. Her outfits made her look half a rock star and half some ethereal fairy queen.

In a word, mystical.

She commanded the audience like a benevolent ruler, earning cheers and whistles with each illusion. He had watched her cross between two closed cages, sixty feet apart, in the blink of an eye; seen her burn away her own gloved hand in front of a gasping crowd, only for it to appear good as new the next moment. Then came the mentalism, predictions and assertions she couldn't possibly know only to be confirmed from within sealed envelopes or from notes in the audience member's pockets. If Greer didn't know any better he might be convinced of some psychic power behind the acts.

But what set Sophie apart was her hypnotism. He'd seen it himself. The first case they'd worked together, then again with his own daughter. Sophie had a gift for opening her target's mind, a skill she had refined until it was as sharp as a surgeon's scalpel.

With the pocketwatch laid on the interrogation table in front of them, Greer leaned back. Anything he did now would only get in her way.

"We're going to take a moment to relax; catch our breath," Sophie said calmly, her words riding the beat of the softly ticking watch.

As she continued to speak, Greer could feel his own pulse slowing, a calm beginning to settle into his muscles. He knew what was happening, blinking hard, he reflexively tensed his legs and arms, fighting not to be lulled in by Sophie's words as she spent the next minute easing Sharpe towards the same sort of trance he'd seen in other suspects.

"You have a cut on your head," Sophie asked. "How did you get it?"

Greer looked closely. He hadn't seen it hidden under Sharpe's dark hair, but now that Sophie had called it out, he could follow a dark scab of dried blood from the top of Sharpe's forehead across his scalp.

"I grabbed her," Sharpe replied softly.

"Your wife?" Sophie urged gingerly.

Sharpe nodded, touching a finger to the brittle scab. "I grabbed her, and she hit me. Smashed a bowl over my head. She fought to the end, so I had to overpower her, to hold her down and... and..." His words drifted off, simply mouthing the final phrase *cut her neck.*

But that didn't make sense. There was no blood on the carpet. If Josephine had hit her husband with a bowl, there would be broken pieces, but the only shattered item they found was the dropped wine glass.

Sharpe's cuffs clinked at the table's edge. He leaned forward, running his palms over his face, up over his forehead, and through his dark hair. His leg was shaking, his heel giving the floor a rapid-fire tap that clashed with the ticking watch.

"It's ok. You can rest your leg," Sophie prompted.

Abruptly, Sharpe pulled at the hair on his head, smacking at his forehead and scalp with a sharp, pained moan. He lunged across the table, his hand coming up for Sophie's throat.

Greer stood so quickly that his own chair shot backward and landed with a loud clang on the concrete floor. In the same motion, he grabbed his partner's shoulders, pulling Sophie back with a protective twist that put him between her and the Sharpe.

The cuffs clanged as Sharpe's wrists snapped short, pushing his sleeves up his arms as he landed face-first on the metal table.

"Stop that! Stop messing with me! I've told you everything you need to hear." Tears streamed down his face as Sharpe lay crumpled on the cold tabletop. "End it. Please. Just end it."

Tapping Greer's shoulder, Sophie tilted her head to the door and the pair retreated.

As Greer shut the door, he realized he still had one arm protectively wrapped around Sophie's shoulder. They were safe, out of the interrogation room, but he didn't let go. She was shaking.

For a moment, Greer simply stood there. Holding her with one arm, he gave her shoulder a light squeeze, though, in the moment, he couldn't say why. He was a protector. He always had been. But something about feeling that shiver running through Sophie... a small twinge of heartache pulled in his chest, alongside a sudden wrathful desire to excuse himself and 'instruct' Mr. Sharpe on proper table manners.

"I couldn't hypnotize him," Sophie said, blinking rapidly as she stared into the middle distance. "There's something in his mind, something so violently insistent that he can't be coaxed down. Not yet. Pain. Fear. A need to be punished... and I don't know what to make of it."

Greer listened, giving her shoulder another pat, letting her lean against him, if only slightly.

Sophie let out a deep sigh through her nose. But in that breath, the shudder left her body, and she was calm and still as she ever had been.

With an almost bashful smile, Sophie mouthed 'thank you', and gave Greer an open palmed pat over his heart as she pulled away from him.

Clearing his throat, Greer murmured, "You're welcome," and removed his arm, suddenly unsure what to do with his hand as he alternated it between his hip and his neck.

"Did you see his arms?" Sophie said.

Greer looked to the interrogation room door, puzzled. "No. Good work catching that cut on his head, though. I hadn't seen that either."

"His wife didn't do that," Sophie said quickly. "And under his shirt, there were bruises on his arms, pressure marks. I think he was tied down."

"So if someone tied him up and killed his wife, why is he confessing?"

Sophie only shook her head. "I still don't know."

"Wait." Greer thought back to the crime scene, to the spilled wine. "We need a tox screen on Sharpe," he said, pulling his cell phone to fire off the request as he started up the police station hallway.

"What are you thinking?" Sophie asked.

"There's certain cocktails, drug mixes, that interrogators use to break people. They're illegal, war crimes even, but they exist. You drug someone up, put them under a light, and if you hammer them hard enough, long enough, you can make them believe anything you want. Make them *do* anything you want." Greer glanced back, pointing a thumb Sophie's way. "If you're right and the victim was drugged—"

"Then maybe whoever killed Josephine is forcing Sharpe to take the fall," Sophie finished for him.

"Come on," Greer said, frowning back to his phone. "I just got the word that the medical examiner has the preliminary done on Ms. Ramsey. We can see about that and put in the request in person."

Chapter 4

The beauty of a death is that it might be anyone's death, the Mask mused to himself.

Just as the beauty of a city is in the way it might be *any* city. Oh, the scenery may change, but the stories were the same. From Troy to Boston. Humans being humans. Peaceful, passionate, brutal, bloody humans.

Grinning, the Mask did a little twirl as he turned the corner, letting the heel of his shoe grind on the cracked concrete. The other people walking the urban streets on the fringes of Baton Rouge paid him no mind. Perhaps they sensed that he was of a higher order, or perhaps he had already transcended beyond their ability to perceive him. He held his hands in his pockets and smiled at the feeling of the sun on his face. The clouds were breaking up, the morning drizzle had dissipated, and he had the extremely good fortune to find himself trailing behind a beautiful young woman.

A block ago, she had lowered her jacket hood, letting flowing locks of raven-black hair loose, her upturned, celestial nose and full lips as lovely in the decayed, urban edges of Louisiana as they might be in a Renaissance portrait or a Grecian urn.

The man's breath caught as she glanced back, his heart racing while he pretended to check his wristwatch, another kind of mask. A mask of casual indifference. "Oh, she doth teach the torches to burn bright," he murmured to himself as soft as a prayer.

Following her had been different from the others, the Mask thought to himself. She's nervous. Eyes always darting. She doesn't follow a routine or stick to the same routes. No, this nineteen-year-old nymph *expects* she's being watched, that she's being followed.

Perhaps the danger even excites her, he thought with a self-satisfied grin.

The secrecy. The lies.

When he began his work, the Mask assumed it would take years. Months between each story. But no, he should have known better. It was the human condition to be frail. To fall to temptation. It was only natural that he should find several, dozens even, sitting on the very precipice of destiny, at the turning point between the plain, ordinary fate of so many and true greatness... true elevation.

He had only just finished a story the evening before, and he was already hungry to begin another.

The young lady abruptly darted into an alleyway.

The Mask smiled, turning around, jogging away from the alleyway to the previous street. He turned left, running parallel to the alley the nubile girl had turned down. She very seldom doubled back, but when she did, she liked to use alleyways for the purpose.

Pulling off his jacket, the Mask reversed it and pulled a folded baseball cap from the inner pocket, shaking it out and setting it squarely on his head.

A car honked at him, and the Mask jumped back to avoid being clipped as he passed the exit of a parking garage.

He smiled and waved as the man inside flipped him the bird and peeled away.

Now there was a man who would meet a tragic end, the Mask thought. A fate he wouldn't need to lift a finger to guide.

When he reached the street corner, the Mask paused, looking up as if considering which way to go. And right on cue, the dark-haired beauty exited an alley mouth, not seven feet from him.

The man looked left and right.

She was so close. He would have sworn he could smell the rose blossoms in her body wash.

He turned toward her, pretending to look to the end of the street beyond her.

It would be such a simple thing. To grab the young woman now, to pull her into the alleyway. A true tragedy. The sacrificial virgin in the den of the dragon. A tale far, far older than Baton Rouge, than Louisiana, or even the first European settlers of these shores.

Only a few steps now.

The Mask's hand twitched, temptation beating in his chest.

The girl didn't even look at him.

His hand rose.

Suddenly she bolted, her raven hair flapping up behind her, a few delicate strands passing between his fingers.

The Mask stopped, looking up to watch the girl run a few dozen yards up the street and leap into the arms of a clean-faced young man. His arms were leanly muscled and his white teeth revealed themselves in a golden smile as he took her by the waist and spun her in his arms.

The girl squealed in delight as the boy pulled her close, her legs locking around his waist. He kissed her. First, kissing her neck, then her cheek, and finally, as she grabbed his dark, thick curls, their lips met.

The Mask sighed.

In his mind's eyes, they seemed to glow with a heavenly light.

Then the girl's skin began to sag. Her raven hair grew thin as lines of silver grey emerged from within. Her tight curves drooped as the boy's flat stomach bulged out in a beer belly, his clean face sprouting over with unkempt whiskers as the thick curls of his head slipped away to reveal a bald pate.

The hallucination faded as the young man lowered his love to the ground. They were whispering soft cautions to each other about being caught. He didn't need to hear them again to know they were worrying over what their friends would think if they knew. What her father would do if someone saw them together. The young woman put her hood back up.

A waste.

All of it will go to waste.

The thought made him angry. Turning bitterly to the wall, the Mask tapped a clenched fist against the brickwork. Frustration boiled up, making his cheeks flush. Turning into the alleyway, he removed his ballcap. They would take the long way to avoid being seen. So he knew he would have no trouble beating them to the young man's meager, one-room apartment.

"In fair Louisiana, we set our scene," he murmured, letting out a manic giggle, "For here's much to do with hate, but more with love."

Chapter 5

"I put in the rush on Sharpe's tox screening as soon as I got your message, but it's not magic. It still takes time."

Dr. Miranda Walsh, a woman built like a brick house with a 'fresh out of medical school' youth to her features, gave a sympathetic shrug as she turned and pulled the morgue drawer open, sliding Josephine Ramsey's body out for viewing. Despite the modesty sheet, Sophie noticed Greer reflexively look away, blinking and taking a breath before turning back to face the body. The Medical Examiner uncovered the victim's pale, bloodless face and lifted her arms from under the cover.

"We appreciate you giving Mr. Sharpe's screening priority anyway," Sophie replied.

Dr. Walsh waved away the comment. rolling her neck and settling her red hair, tied back in a ponytail, over one shoulder. "Happy to help," she said in a tone that told Sophie that, at best, she was coolly resigned to help.

As Sophie adjusted the light over the body, Walsh's eyes narrowed and she raised one finger, letting it bob in the air a moment before settling into an angle vaguely in Sophie's direction. "Have we met before?"

Sophie nipped her lower lip for a moment, suddenly feeling a touch sheepish. She remembered this freezing autopsy room clearly. It was the room where she'd first met Greer. Her eyes flitted to the hazardous waste bin by the door and the cup of coffee in Greer's hand. Midday had passed and she had had no objection when he stopped for a caffeine break on the drive over.

"We have," Sophie replied noncommittally, then, when it seemed clear that Dr. Walsh was not about to continue without an explanation, Sophie cleared her throat. "I, uh, impersonated you a couple weeks ago... in this room. The Copycat Killer case?"

Dr. Walsh snapped her fingers, a bright smile revealing rosy dimples in her cheeks. "Yes, I remember now." She turned to Greer, "You were *soooo* confused. I remember you had the funniest look on your face. Just pure shock." The red-headed ME covered her mouth to suppress a laugh.

Despite the situation, and the dead body between them, Sophie found herself smiling along with Dr. Walsh. The woman clearly had a good sense of humor about the whole situation.

"Well now, Agent Greer, if you get confused again, you can just check my name tag, right here." Leaning forward, Walsh tapped the little copper nameplate on her chest, and Sophie watched as Greer's cheeks immediately blushed over.

With a cough, the handsome, older agent looked away. "Sure thing, Miss Walsh—Doctor Walsh. My apologies."

Sophie tilted her head a fraction of an inch, her smile freezing for less than a second. Something in Dr. Walsh's eyes. A slight dilation, her look lingering after Greer met her eyes and looked away...

Hurrying the moment along, Sophie put her hands on the edge of the morgue table. "So what can you tell us?"

Dr. Walsh reluctantly looked away from Greer and reached down to lift up the victim's arm. "The slash on her throat is the cause of death," she said casually. "No surprise there. We found a bruise on her hip that may indicate a struggle, as well as these bruises on her arms."

Showing Josephine Ramsey's bare forearms, Sophie could see—a few inches above the wrist, where the sleeves of her professional blouse would have covered—Josephine's arms had two bruises, less than an inch thick, draped like halves of a bracelet over the tops of her forearms.

"She was tied to the chair?" Sophie asked, genuine surprise creeping into her voice.

"I believe so. But the reports didn't mention bindings on her wrists," Dr. Walsh prompted.

"There weren't any," Greer confirmed. "She was untied when the housekeeper discovered the body. At least, that was her statement."

Dr. Walsh circled the exam table, stepping between Sophie and Greer to reach the other arm. Sophie tried not to read any more into the choice, but as Dr. Walsh angled her shoulder to face a few degrees toward Greer, Sophie found her lips drawing into an impatient line.

"See here," Walsh said, lifting the bruised arm for Greer, and presumably Sophie, to get a look at. Greer lifted a finger, squinting close as he pointed to the arc of the bruise.

"There's no ray pattern," Greer said curiously. "She didn't struggle when she was tied up."

"Precisely." Smiling, Walsh reached up to point at the bruised arm as well. "We would expect friction abrasions and additional lines of bruising if she was struggling against them, but there are none here."

As the medical examiner indicated her point, her hand brushed against Greer's. Chuckling awkwardly, he pulled his hand back, stuffing it into the pocket of his tan suit.

"That's consistent with her being drugged," Sophie said. As she spoke, she realized the words came out flat, almost combative. Clearing her throat, she said more pleasantly. "Did you have a tox screen for the victim?"

"Yes," Dr. Walsh replied, gingerly setting down the arm and plucking a manila folder from the countertop across from them. "We found sedatives. Rohypnol, roofies," she elaborated. "And they match the samples from the Maya Rossi case. Both women were drugged before they were killed."

"Why tie her up then?" Greer puzzled, flipping through the report.

"It could be symbolic," Sophie offered. "Or maybe it was just to keep her from falling out of her chair. He removed them afterward so they must not be important to whatever tableau the killer is trying to create."

"The killer?" Dr. Walsh asked, raising an eyebrow. "I'm confused. I thought her husband confessed, just like in the Rossi case."

"He did," Sophie confirmed. "But it's strange. Too convenient. Too odd. His behavior doesn't match his claim. We think he has bruising on his arms just like the victim's too."

"You think he was also tied up?" Walsh interjected. "And then what? He escaped? The real killer let him go, and he rushed to the police to confess the crime anyway?"

Sophie bit her lip, her chin rising slightly as she sucked in a quick breath. "Maybe. I know it sounds far-fetched, but when we brought up Rossi, he looked... confused. Then started to claim he'd killed her as well."

"Did anyone run a tox screen on James Rossi, the first victim's husband?" Greer asked.

Walsh shook her head. "No. When he confessed, it seemed open and shut. He was remorseful, upset, but the detectives in charge didn't see any reason to suspect he'd been drugged or coerced. And if I'm honest, neither do I." With a huff and a resigned flare of her eyebrows, Walsh said, "Like I said, I pushed Mr. Sharpe's tox screen. But I think it's going to come back negative."

"Why do you say that?" Greer asked.

Dr. Walsh gave a jokingly smug grin, waggling her eyebrows, "Because in cases like this, nine times out of ten, the husband did it. You say he had bruises, but if he fell against a table or his wife tried to fight back, he could get linear bruising a few different ways."

"You sound confident," Greer added skeptically. "No chance you're wrong?"

Walsh lifted one shoulder with a carefree tilt of her head. "I'll bet you dinner that I'm not," she teased.

Sophie's spine stiffened with annoyance. She felt a sharp retort forming in her mouth, but instead, she blinked, swallowing the impulse. It was just teasing, maybe a bit unprofessional, but since when had Sophie Quinn cared about people flirting with their coworkers? Why did she care?

Because it's not two stagehands sneaking into the sound booth to blow off some steam, she thought. It's Greer. He... well, he's saved your life... Was that it? Was she getting flustered because another woman was flirting with the man who rescued her? What did that mean? She could feel her mind getting muddled as it became harder and harder to deny that she had been developing a little crush on the handsome, older agent with the crystal blue eyes.

When she looked up, Sophie found Greer's face fully turning red as he scratched at the back of his head and gave a nervous chuckle. Sophie remembered what he had told her in the bayou during their last case. How his wife had vanished ten years ago, leaving him to raise his daughter, Kinsley, alone. He'd joked about Kinsley's attempts to get him back into the dating scene, but from his reaction to Walsh's suggestions... had he really not been on a date in a decade?

Tucking his palms into his elbows, Greer gave a tight-lipped smile, clearly trying to move on from the mild flirtation. "No, I think I might lose that bet," he said to Walsh. "What you said makes sense. But it's strange..."

Refocusing, and closing her eyes to her own small sigh of relief at Greer's reaction, Sophie nodded along with her partner's answer. A few hours ago, she had thought the same thing, but now the coincidences were adding up. Two killings with the same pattern. Two remorseful husbands who both confessed the day after. Both within a few days of each other.

Expectation is the enemy of observation. The phrase rose in Sophie's mind as it so often did when she felt she'd hit a wall in her thinking. Knowing what was typical was helpful, to a point. They say that when you hear hoofbeats, you should think *horses* and not *zebras*. And despite what the last few weeks told her, serial killers were rarely compared to the everyday sort of murderer... the crimes of passion, killings over money or sex.

But this...

Sophie glanced at Greer. He looked pensive, running a calloused hand over the light stubble on his chin. His middle finger unconsciously traced a centimeter-long scar on the left side of his jaw.

"Something has to connect them," Greer said grimly. "Someone has to be behind the murders. If both husbands lied. There *will* be another killing."

"But if there's someone else behind it, why leave the husbands alive?" Sophie said with a sigh. "Why make them confess? And *how?* Is the real killer genuinely expecting to deflect the blame or is this just another layer to the game they are playing? Is the false confession supposed to tell us something?"

With a sigh, Dr. Walsh folded her arms. "Look. I know that you're going to have to do your due diligence, but sometimes—"

With a chirp, the ME's phone flashed, and she cut off her thought as she picked it up. "Huh," she said softly, frowning as she tapped the screen. "Well, Agent Greer. It looks like you're off the hook for that dinner."

Chapter 6

Meeting with the Sharpe family brought several phrases to Sophie's mind. But she quickly settled on hornet's nest. Yes, a hornet's nest would be a good way to describe the experience of entering the modest, split-level home south-east of the city.

Noisy, busy, and furious.

But Jonathan Sharpe had been drugged, just like his wife. And if someone was trying to frame him for murder... well, his family was as good a place to start as any.

The yard was overgrown at the edges and a homemade birdhouse hung on one nail from a lonely fencepost, grey and decrepit from age and casting a long shadow from the late afternoon sun. But the windows were clean and the driveway was swept, giving Sophie a view of the storm within before they even knocked.

After a young woman unlatched the screen door to let them in—Jonathan Sharpe's younger sister Nora as they quickly learned—no less than seven members of the family, ages seventeen to seventy, surrounded her and Agent Greer. Various demands to 'take off their shoes', 'come sit down', and 'tell me why the hell my son is in jail' were dropped with equal vehemence and perplexing aggression as an old woman in a sundress, Sharpe's mother she guessed, grabbed Greer by the shoulders and pushed him into the living room, seeming not to care if Sophie followed or not.

The family patriarch, a bowling ball of a man wearing brown, leather suspenders and a white shirt bloomed over with the day's sweat, adjusted his glasses to better glare down at Sophie. "My son's wife is dead, and you have the gall to lock him up like he's some—some murderer! I demand you let him out. Now!"

Before either she or Greer could reply, a man wearing a plain white undershirt, loosely concealed by a plaid button-up, let out a bark of a laugh. "Pop, if you don't think Jon-boy put the knife to that witch of his, you're crazy."

Sharpe's brother. Sophie would have guessed the man to be in his forties, and she could see a bald patch as he turned away and took a gulp of the beer in his hand.

"Goddamnit, Ricky, you shut the hell up!" the old man snapped. his voice already hoarse in a way that told Sophie this wasn't the first time he'd shouted today.

Ricky, of course, did not shut up. Instead, letting out a belch and calling over his shoulder, "He confessed, Pop. And good for him, finally staked that vampire—"

He never finished the thought, as the woman in the sundress reeled back and slapped him across the cheek. The sudden motion setting the beer in his hand fizzing as he stumbled back.

Putting his fingers to his lips, Greer let out a sharp whistle that drove all other sounds from the room. All eyes turned to them, and the agent lifted his palm like a trainer holding an unruly hound to heel.

"Thank you for agreeing to speak with us. I'm Agent Greer; this is FBI Consultant Quinn. We're investigating all possibilities in this case, so we'd like to ask you some questions about Jonathan Sharpe and his wife. We'd like to keep this as civil as possible," he shot a meaningful glance to Ricky alternately holding his beer to his stung cheek as he continued to drain the can. "And we won't take any more of your time than we have to," Greer finished, propping his hands on his hips.

"You mean you want everyone to shut up and play nice," Ricky said with a bitter bite. He let out a mirthless chuckle. "Good luck."

A second young woman in blue jeans and a halter top let out a disgusted sound, "Ricky will you just shut up for five goddamn minutes?"

Greer raised a hand to call for silence again, but if the gathered family saw, they didn't show it, and the room began to boil again with inarticulate insults and sharp words driving out the previous silence. Greer stepped toward Ricky, harsh words exchanged as the man laughed in the agent's face.

This was getting them nowhere.

Sophie took a deep breath, letting her eyes harden. Her chin rose, her posture a bit straighter now as she stepped to the fireplace. Hardly a stage, but it was an empty spot that drew the eye, the hard stone of the chimney creating a focal point she could use.

"Everyone." Sophie's voice commanded the room just as she'd done for years on the stage. The FBI consultant retreated and she let the character of the mysterious, powerful magician come forward. Her footing, her posture, the roll of her shoulders, and the flash of her eyes subtly told the room she was in control.

First one voice went quiet then another, until all eyes were on her. She let a small, dissatisfied twist appear in the corner of her lips, not enough to come across as condescending, so slender that many probably wouldn't even know they'd seen it, but enough to send the signal, the animal intuition that they had made a mistake.

"We can have a conversation here," she gestured around the room. "It won't take long, and then you're free to do whatever you like. Or we can take you one by one to the police station for a formal interrogation." Here she held up two fingers, emphasizing the choice she was giving them. "The decision is yours. But there has been a murder and, by God, we *will* have answers. Lives are at stake, and you *will not* waste our time. Have I made myself clear?"

A silent heartbeat passed in the room, eyes lowered, heads turned away in shame or smothered embarrassment. Sophie nodded, taking the quiet for agreement to her terms.

A timid voice from the entryway was the first to speak. Nora, the young woman who let them in. "Is it true?" she asked. "Did Jonny really confess?" Her fingers were worrying at the hem of her blouse, an off-the-rack, sleeveless piece in white and rose with a simple floral pattern.

"He did," Sophie said gently, letting the fire out of her voice. "But," holding up a hand to ward off interruption, she added, "there are details that don't add up yet." Sophie briefly considered letting the family know that their kin had been drugged and possibly intimidated into confessing, but the room was already a powder keg. Instead, she said, "If he's not being truthful, we're hoping to get a better picture of why. If there's any possibility someone else committed this crime, we're going to explore it and find out."

Ricky scoffed.

"You have something to tell us?" Sophie prompted. She turned her body to fully face the balding man with the beer.

He rolled his eyes, smirking as he took another drink. Sophie continued to stare at him as his eyes flitted to her then away. By inches, his smug grin turned to a frown as his discomfort at her unyielding stare grew. Finally, he let out a grunt, gesturing around the room with the dregs of his beer.

"Everyone here is going to pretend like Jonny's some kind of saint just because he's kin. He's not."

"You watch your mouth, Rick Sharpe," the old man in suspenders growled.

"Sir," Greer took a step towards the man, holding up a palm. The old man batted the gesture away, sinking into an arm chair as he glowered at his adult son.

"What do you mean by that?" Sophie said, keeping her eyes fixed on Ricky.

"I mean that Jon-boy's the type of man to do whatever it takes to get what he wants. He doesn't care who he hurts."

The woman in the sundress stepped to her husband, putting a calming hand on his shoulder. But out of the corner of her eye, Sophie could see the way her own jaw was set, clenched as her lips quivered with unspoken argument.

"Was there someone that Mr. Sharpe had hurt?" Sophie asked. "Someone who may want to make him suffer? Maybe someone able to blackmail him over what he'd done?"

Ricky shrugged. "I don't know any details. I just know that's the way Jonny's always been. We had a business together, years ago, and he cut me out. When he was ready to move on to his *next big thing,* he didn't sell the business back to me, he just liquidated the whole damn thing. He's a shark. A pirate," He gave a bitter snort and tried to take another sip of his beer, finding it empty. "Josephine was perfect for him. He was a dick and she was bitch."

Sophie caught a couple of the other family members silently nodding while still others had gone unnaturally still.

"They were a power couple," Nora said, her voice squeaking. "And they loved each other."

Ricky sneered. "If you want to call it that. Looked to me like they just got off on being rich together. You saw them at the barbeque."

"The barbeque?" Sophie asked, pulling Ricky's attention back from his younger sister.

The old man grunted from his chair. "Last weekend," he said. "Family and friends. Jonny and his wife are always welcome, though they don't always come."

"You mean they almost never come," Ricky said. "Just flaunting that new car of theirs. Showing off. Last time, Josephine made Anabelle cry."

"She's Jonny's cousin," Ricky's mother interjected.

"Jonny took his wife a pace away over by the shed after that. I hoped maybe he'd talk her into apologizing to the poor girl, and the next thing I know, the vampire and Jon-boy are sucking tongue in front of God and everybody. That seem like love to you, Nora?"

"Rick!" his father said, knuckles white on the arm chair.

"I don't always understand them, but I know Jonny. He talked to me," Nora said, her words half-drowned by a slurred insult from her brother. "He wouldn't kill anyone," she said pathetically. Sophie only heard it because she was already on her way to Nora's side.

The living room was teetering on the edge of another shouting match, and Sophie shot a quick glance to Greer, nodding toward the back-door as she muttered, "Barbeque," under her breath.

Greer nodded, giving a quick, sharp clap. "Alright, hold on. I want to know more about this fight at the barbeque. Everyone to the back yard, show me what happened and where."

"Oh, this'll be rich," Ricky grunted.

"Just because you were too drunk to remember where you were," the blue-jeaned young woman hissed.

"Enough," Greer warned. "Come on. Everyone."

In a wave of disgruntled shifting, the Sharpe family filtered to the kitchen and out the back patio door, jostling and whispering cutting words to each other the whole way.

As the herd started moving, Sophie gently grabbed Nora's elbow. "Miss, would you mind hanging back a moment," she asked. "I have a few questions about what you said."

Nora gave a puzzled look, glancing uncertainly between Sophie and her departing family, but then nodded and folded her hands until the room was empty.

Sophie thought about what the young woman had just said. Taking a moment to put a sympathetic hand on her shoulder. "I'm sorry for what you're going through," she said. "It sounds like you and Jonny are close."

She nodded, looking at the carpet.

Sophie stepped back, settling on the arm of a plush chair and crossing her ankle casually. This seemed to relax the younger woman, and she also took a seat, her shoulders loosening and her lungs easing enough to let out a long sigh.

"He's not a killer," she said softly.

Sophie could feel a 'but' coming and gave Nora the moment she needed to realize no one was going to contradict her.

"But Jonny and Josephine... well, they are built different. I hate it when Ricky says it, but... well, they are..."

"Sharks," Sophie finished.

Nora nodded, blinking at tears threatening the corner of her eyes. "Jonny and I have always been close. We talk about everything. And he and Josephine, it's like they think of themselves like a king and queen. It was really weird when he first told me, but I didn't judge." Suddenly she looked up and met Sophie's eyes, "You're not going to tell anyone what I say to you, right? I know you need-I mean-you need to know about Jonny so you can find the *real* killer, but things are already..."

Embarrassment.

The young woman was smoothing the bottom of her blouse over and over, running her hands over her jeans and leaving just enough of a mark to show her palms were sweating. No great feat in a Louisiana summer, but when combined with the hesitant pinch of her eyebrows... her closed-in posture...

Sophie leaned forward. "I just want to find out who killed Josephine," she said softly. "If you know something... uncomfortable... about Jonny, I won't share it unless I absolutely have to. And I only have to if it catches the real killer."

Nora bit her lower lip, looking around the floor at her feet. Then she leaned toward Sophie as well. "Jonny had access to a lot of money, through his company I mean." Her voice was so low it was nearly a whisper. "He worked stocks, traded in international companies. He said playing the markets was like gambling, and he was very good at gambling. He could read people, manipulate them."

Nora looked around nervously. Sophie could distantly hear Greer wrangling the Sharpe clan in the backyard, barking out like the military man he was as he set about recreating the cookout from the week before. No one else was in the house.

"He said that when he won a lot... whether he closed a big deal or took the pot in a high-stakes poker game, he felt like a king showing off his conquests to his queen. They actually talked like that. He said Josephine thought it was-well... that she thought it was *hot* when he'd win big. He started gambling with money that wasn't his... in places that he shouldn't have been... The Black Coral Club." Nora tilted her head, blinking and sniffling as a tear spilled across her cheek. "I think he might have gotten in trouble with someone there... someone bad.

Someone who might have killed Josephine and made him take the blame."

Sophie's heart was racing. The Black Coral Club had appeared in several of the documents she had pored over across the last half-decade. One of Sophie's early theories about RK had speculated he was a hitman for the Louisiana mob engaging in 'extracurricular activities'. Her PI, Fabian St. Claire, had noted the location many times as a den of vice: prostitution, gambling, drugs, and other parts of the Baton Rouge underworld.

A place one could hire a killer.

If Jonathan Sharpe was involved in the Black Coral Club's backroom games, Sophie had no doubt that the men involved could and would cut his wife's throat over a gambling debt.

But what made Sophie's blood freeze wasn't the connection to the second victim's husband...

Her mind flashed back to what Greer had told her about James Rossi, husband of the first victim—the police report filed for attacking a man outside a club. She could picture it now, the note, the position on the page—the address and name of the club—how odd it had seemed that he hadn't been arrested...

Of course there were no charges filed... the Black Coral Club had their own brand of justice.

Personal. And deadly.

Chapter 7

"This isn't going to work at all," Sophie murmured.

"What? Why?" Greer asked, half a whisper as he looked out through their sedan's windshield.

In answer, Sophie gestured to the former Marine's attire. His typical tan suit was gone. Instead, he wore a white t-shirt under a dark blazer, with sleeves rolled half-way up his toned forearms, blue jeans torn at the knees, and gym shoes. A gaudy ring, the sort a prom king would wear to commemorate a high school football championship, sat on one pinkie finger, and with a tooth-pick dangling between his lips, Greer lowered a pair of aviator sunglasses to meet Sophie's eye line. "I think I look sharp," he said coyly.

"You look like an edgy teen at homecoming," Sophie replied, not unkindly, snatching the toothpick from his mouth and tossing it out the window.

The sound of a gunshot had marked their arrival on Tenpenny Street.

If anyone else heard it, they concealed the fact well. Sophie noted only a few turned heads and perhaps a quickening of pace as a few bar-hoppers and tired-looking men looking to score a fix hurried on their way. But within a minute, the pistol's bark had been forgotten. Just another sound of the night, like crickets in the sparse grass, the scream of frogs from the ditches and canals, or the throbbing pulse of dance music escaping concrete walls.

The sun had set, and the creatures of the night were out.

Tense, like a coiled spring or the cocked hammer of a revolver, Greer looked out over the steering wheel to the violet and red sign of the Black Coral Club, the swinging door seeming to suck in light rather than give it off as people stumbled in and out, some already drunkenly shambling to an alley to relieve their bladders or their stomachs, sometimes both. A couple dozen people stood in line behind an oak tree of a man in a black t-shirt that managed to show off every inch of his gorilla-strong biceps.

The neon glare of Tenpenny Street's bars and nightclubs splashed over Greer's white sedan's windows, falling in stripes and starbursts over Sophie and her partner. She looked over to Greer once again and let out a sigh.

They'd only had half-an-hour to prepare for the club. They had to blend in if they were going to make it to the back rooms, and they couldn't exactly stroll up in the G-men suits they usually wore.

Sophie had a long jacket on over her outfit; the summer air carried a slight chill now that the sun had set. It had seemed so simple an hour ago. But now doubt was setting in.

"You know what'll happen if they find out we're FBI in there?" she said to Greer.

"I do," he said simply. "You're not the only one aware of the Black Coral Club's reputation," he added. There was nothing condescending in his tone. It sounded more like he was trying to reassure her that he'd be ready if things went sideways.

That comforted Sophie, and she found herself unconsciously nodding in response. She carried a stylishly simple, faux-leather clutch and as she squeezed the bottom she felt the grip of her pistol rubbing against a collection of small plastic and clay beads. She pictured the eclectic bracelet, strung with trinkets sent to her from all over the world by her friend and mentor, the Great Gavriel.

"People hear what they see," Sophie said softly, reminding herself of one of the old stage performer's many mantras. "Alright, let's go."

As they approached, the doorman held up a meaty hand. "Line starts back there," he said flatly, twisting a thumb to the dozen or so people forming a crooked conga across the sidewalk.

"We're expected inside," Greer said confidently, his hands in his pockets as he gestured with his thumbs.

"You and everybody else," the doorman grunted. "Line."

Side by side, Sophie saw that the doorman was easily six-six, putting him taller than the leanly muscled agent. And where Greer was athletic, with functional, whipcord muscle, the doorman was three feet from shoulder to shoulder and built like a bull.

"Come on," Greer insisted, taking a step closer to the man. "I'm sure we can—"

"Are you deaf or something? Back of the line—sir."

Seeing the way Greer's eyes narrowed to meet the bouncer's 'you're-starting-to-piss-me-off' stare, Sophie flashed the man a million-dollar smile, her chin tilting in a way that implied he was forgivably mistaken. "I'm sure we're on the list," she said demurely.

Giving Greer another look that told Sophie he seriously doubted her assertion, the double-wide doorman lifted a smartphone, looking down at the screen as he growled, "Name?"

"Quinn," Sophie said with a bubbly delight that she'd last used for talk-shows and press circuits. "Oh, look, there we are!" she quickly added, her hand flying up from her clutch to point at the bouncer's phone screen.

He squinted down to where she was pointing, and as he did, Sophie adjusted her grip, a hundred-dollar bill peeking out from her palm.

There was a tense moment, a heartbeat where nobody moved. Anxiety bruited through Sophie's veins. If this didn't work, they'd be down to breaking and entering. Deciding to venture one last gambit, Sophie whispered, "We're here for the *game,"* Inflecting the word meaningfully as she did.

The bouncer blinked. Another breathless heartbeat.

He made a motion to swipe away the screen on his phone, discretely snatching the bill as he did. "Apologies, Ms. Quinn," he said brusquely. "Enjoy the Black Coral Club."

With a gracious nod, Sophie looped an arm through Greer's elbow, feeling the knot of muscle where he'd been clenching a fist. She gave an animated squeal of delight and hopped up onto her tip-toes, to plant a quick peck on the bouncer's cheek.

The big man rubbed his face in surprise then grinned and jokingly waved Sophie away, the expression abruptly evaporating as he slammed an open palm against another member of the line attempting to slip in with Sophie and Greer.

Sophie didn't see what happened to the other hopeful entrant as the club's doors swung shut behind her.

* * *

"Ok, we're in. You can relax," she said into Greer's ear, patting his bicep, and dropping the girlish mask she'd adopted with the doorman.

Dark lights and swirls of color mixed with trace vapor from a fog machine by the dance floor, and the throbbing music, barely audible outside, now filled their ears.

An island bar surrounded by booths sat on the darker side of the room, and through the mist and strobing light, Sophie could see a cross-section of Baton Rouge's night life decked out in a wild array of outfits, or a distinct lack of attire, filling the booths like samples in a box of chocolates.

The dance floor churned with bodies as the young, the fit, and the beautiful all vied for their slice of the action; arms and legs gyrating, flailing, or nimbly twisting with robotic precision. Sophie remembered this sort of scene all too well. The sweat and the alcohol filling the air until you could hardly breathe; adrenaline and sound; touching, the welcome and unwelcome variety. It was like the whole place was in a blender, everyone and everything mingling... except for the bar. The bar was the Great Wall, where all chaos stopped, and the bartender was like some Greek god, able to send you to bliss or to call down the bouncers like vengeful Furies to smite you.

Sophie couldn't help but be struck in the moment, a memory of the church potluck at her parents' trailer park leaping to her mind. The wholesome clapping to the rhythm of the zydeco band instead of the heart-attack pulse of the DJ; kids racing along the canal paths and grandmothers ladling up gumbo in styrofoam bowls instead of coked-out partiers pawing at each other over colorful liquors.

Her thoughts returned to her father lying unconscious in his hospital bed. She wondered if he'd woken up. Mama would send her a text if he had... right? Sophie checked her phone. No new alerts.

A drunk man with bloodshot eyes stumbled against her, giggling an apology as he steadied his drink and slapping Sophie's butt through her jacket while she and Greer stepped away. She fought down the urge to put him in a wrist lock. First, because they had a job to do and drawing unwanted attention would compromise that, and second, because she'd been around Greer enough to realize if he learned what the man had done, that man wouldn't be leaving here with his head intact: see point one.

Sophie looked around again, trying to pinpoint where the entrance to the backroom games might be. She couldn't find any obvious doorways, apart from the bars and the metal swinging doors leading to a kitchen area near the booths. That might be a possibility.

"Let's get to the bar," Sophie said quickly, tugging Greer along.

They took a seat together, squeezing between the patrons as a man in white face paint and a woman in a neon pink mini-skirt vacated their stools and slipped off to the dance floor. Greer sat straight backed, looking around the room like a Doberman scenting an intruder. Sophie frowned. They'd passed a couple more bouncers on their way across the club floor, and she knew the club's real owners would have precautions in place to look out for cops and their informants.

"Hey," Sophie said, intently leaning forward and putting a palm on the bar. "Don't be so stiff."

"I'm not stiff," Greer replied, continuing to look around. "I'm just here to party, scoping out some babes," he added flatly.

Sophie almost burst out laughing, instead pinching her lips in a suppressed smile. "You look like a dad trying to catch his teenage daughter sneaking out after curfew."

With a groan, Greer rolled his eyes and waved to the bartender. A few moments later, he accepted a tumbler of whiskey as Sophie took a glass of red wine. He leaned forward on the bar, his eyes darting right and left as he took a sip of his drink.

Sophie took the moment to make some small talk with the young woman on her right. Cindy. Going into nursing. An old break on her left hand's pinkie finger. Not that this last detail came up in their conversation, it was simply something Sophie clocked as the young woman took a sip of her beer. In the several minutes they talked, Sophie noted several members of the staff coming and going through the kitchen doors behind Cindy, but no one who looked dressed to enter a high-stakes gambling den. She'd have to watch longer to be sure, but it was looking less likely by the minute.

As Cindy got up and disappeared from her life, Sophie turned back to Greer, who was still coiled over the bar, his head turning like a security camera as he nursed his drink.

"Kitchen door doesn't look likely," she said.

He nodded, then gestured with his drink. "There's an office behind one-way glass over the dance floor. Doesn't seem likely either. I'm guessing it's accessed through a back entrance, maybe through the kitchen area. I don't see an elevator or stairs."

Sophie caught the bartender's eye; even several yards away, he was giving Greer a disappointed frown as he wiped the glass in his hand and served up another patron. Sophie could understand why.

"Come on," she said quickly. "You're drawing attention."

"How?" he asked incredulously, "I'm just sitting here."

"Exactly." Sophie propped an elbow on the bar, raising an eyebrow as she looked him over. "You are believable as a sad drunk here to drown your sorrows, but we're in a nightclub. Wrong energy."

"Ouch," Greer said, grinning and sitting back upright.

Now that they'd been in here a while, the body heat of the claustrophobic press of people around them was starting to make Sophie feel stifled in her jacket. She took it off, folding it over her arm and revealing the slim, black dress she'd chosen. The spaghetti straps exposed her shoulders, and the sleek fabric hugged her body from her chest down to mid-thigh, yet she was definitely *not* wearing the most revealing outfit in the room. Though, by the stunned look Greer gave her, for a moment she felt as if she were.

His clear, blue eyes shot wide and she saw the poor man struggle for a moment as they instinctively flitted down over her and then back to his whiskey. Jonathan Greer, ever the gentleman.

"Flirt with me," Sophie quickly interjected.

Greer sputtered in his glass, then tilted his head, glancing at the half-full glass of red wine next to Sophie.

"Don't overthink it," she said, leaning forward so they wouldn't be overheard. As she did, she put a hand on Greer's chest. "You're here with me. That's the cover." Giving him a coy grin, she inclined her head, letting her auburn hair touch her bare shoulder. "Over my shoulder, you can see the kitchen entrance and the east wall. I can see the west side of the house behind you. And no one will care if we're slow on our drinks if we're... involved."

Sophie slipped her hand down from Greer's chest, across his arm, and took his hand. They had the roughness of a man with a history of hard work, gym callouses and patterns from hours at the pistol range keeping his skills sharp. Her own hands were strong in different ways, thousands of days' worth of training, catching and manipulating playing cards, darts, and the endless variety of objects her work as an illusionist demanded.

Even so... they felt—small—almost delicate in Greer's coarse yet gentle hands.

He twisted on his stool, not letting go of her hand as he faced her full-on. His eyes still hovered awkwardly as if unsure where to look.

"So..." he said at last, "come here often?"

Sophie let out a bright laugh, taking her wine in her other hand as she shook her head sympathetically. "You really are out of practice, aren't you?"

Greer chuckled along with her, nodding softly. "Yeah... I suppose I am," he said.

Their eyes met once more and as Sophie looked past Greer, scanning the far side of the room, she said, "I take it, no time in the schedule for hot dates as a single dad and FBI agent?"

With a click of the tongue, Greer replied, "That's about the sum of it." Then, more seriously, he added, "After Margo left, I had to focus on Kinsley. And myself. I told you some of it. I couldn't let myself backslide. I had to be the best father I could, for her."

Sophie thought of her walk with Greer through the bayou during their last case, how he'd told her about his wife's addiction problem, how she abandoned him and Kinsley. It was heartbreaking, particularly after the time Sophie had spent with the pair.

"I guess," Greer continued. "I guess I got used to the idea or thought, you know, that if someone did come along, I'd just keep an open mind. I guess no one did."

Sophie softly squeezed his hand. "No one? Not one person shot their shot with a handsome, sensitive man with a great job and a house in the suburbs?" It was half a joke, an instinctive line to lighten the mood.

But Sophie noticed as she spoke, Greer's thumb was idly tracing the back of her knuckles.

She didn't react, didn't look down. Maybe it was the wine or the way her whole life had become a gauntlet of pain and serial murderers over the last few weeks, but in that moment, as the words left her lips, she felt secretly grateful that no one had taken their chance with the handsome agent.

Greer's eyes focused back on Sophie.

His thumb abruptly stopped, and Sophie saw a flush of color rise in the agent's face. He gently pulled his hand away. But Sophie caught it, her index finger curling and catching the last knuckle of his, leaving them linked.

She leaned forward, her other hand moving to Greer's knee.

"Excuse me, Miss Quinn."

The clear, crisp voice of the bartender cut through the noise and Sophie nearly fell out of her stool as she took a sharp breath and sat back up, Greer likewise pulled his hands back to the bar top.

The bartender gave no sign that he cared about or even noticed what he'd interrupted. God, what had he interrupted? Sophie thought wildly. But she didn't have time to think as the young man continued, "We appreciate you visiting The Black Coral Club. Mr. De Soto would like to invite you and your companion to the VIP area if you'd care to accompany Victor."

Sophie's heart plummeted into her stomach. They'd been noticed. She hadn't thought about giving her real name at the door, but now she couldn't help but fixate on the way the young man said it.

Like a shadow out of a nightmare, the broad-shouldered bouncer from the front stepped beside them, his hands folded neatly at his waist. "Right this way, Miss Quinn."

Chapter 8

Sophie steeled herself, letting an easy expression settle on her lips and keeping her head high. For all she knew, she and Greer were being led to their execution in the basement of the Black Coral Club.

The mountain of a bouncer, Victor, led them to the back of a private dining room, to a velvet panel in the wall that opened with a push to reveal a transparent door of what looked to Sophie like bullet-proof glass. On the other side, two silent men built like NFL linemen stood at the ready in expensive suits and holding MP5 submachine guns.

It was exactly the sort of set up Sophie would expect from a vice lord like Henry De Soto.

As they approached, Greer's posture shifted, solidifying his stance, readying himself for danger. It told her all she needed to know. The former Marine took these men as a genuine threat and not simple goons with guns.

One of the men stepped forward, settling his weapon and gesturing for Greer to spread his arms.

For a tense moment, he didn't move, and Victor gave a nervous chuckle as the mob soldier with the machine gun frowned.

"I'm afraid visitors to the VIP room must submit to a pat-down, friend," the bouncer said firmly but professionally.

Greer didn't move.

"It's alright." Sophie quickly put a hand on Greer's shoulder, giving him a meaningful look. "We're not expecting any trouble."

This was, of course, not precisely true. But if they didn't get *into the room,* any trouble they found would be a moot point. Then again, she still didn't know why the mobster and club owner had called them in. But judging by the polite professionalism, it wasn't exactly feeling like a trap...

With a grim exhalation, Greer widened his stance, holding up his arms parallel to the floor as Sophie stepped back. The guard gave him several bracing pats across his arms, hips, and legs. And as he reached Greer's back, Sophie heard the dull *fwap* of his hefty hand hitting the hard leather of Greer's concealed holster.

"No guns in the VIP room," the guard said flatly, leaving the implication for Greer to act on.

Gritting his teeth, he shot Sophie a final look then lifted his shirt tail. A compact Glock came free and as he held it out, grip-first, Victor supplied a small plastic box to deposit it.

Satisfied, the mob soldier turned to face Sophie.

Her face a mask of pleasant acceptance, she concealed the spike of anxiety as she thought about her own pistol concealed in her clutch. As they'd entered the room, she'd hidden the clutch in the fold of her jacket, now held to one side, but any determined search would absolutely find the pistol.

Her sleek dress didn't have sleeves or pockets for her to conceal anything, but she was still surprised when the guard didn't take the opportunity to frisk her as enthusiastically as he had Greer. Instead, he produced a discrete metal detector and began to wand it over her body. Sophie supposed this spoke well of De Soto's view of female visitors to his games.

But still, having both her and Greer disarmed...

Sophie shifted onto her left foot, the closest she'd get to betraying her fear as she made a choice.

"I'm impressed by Mr. De Soto's security," she said, a little loudly for the narrow checkpoint.

"Thank you, Miss Quinn. We try our best," Victor replied genially.

A brief phrase, but the words had done their work. The guard with the wand's attention had been split for a narrow moment. Just as he was shifting to check Sophie's other side, she changed her coat, and the hidden clutch, over to her other arm. The wand and hidden clutch circled Sophie's body in opposite directions, hidden from each other by her casual misdirection as she cheekily joked, "I can't imagine anyone trying anything with a greeting like this."

Victor chuckled. "Not often—though—well, they do *try.*" The other mob soldiers grinned along with this as the one with the metal detector stepped back.

"Clean," he said briskly as he retreated to the edge of the room.

Sophie and Greer walked forward together, expecting Victor to lead them into the next room when the bouncer held up a hand.

"One moment." With an apologetic smile, he stepped in front of Sophie. "I'm sorry, but I have to check your purse." And tilting his head, he motioned with his eyes to the jacket in Sophie's arms.

Sophie felt her heart stop.

Greer stiffened beside her, hurriedly saying, "Come on, we've just been through the metal detector. Do you really want to keep your boss waiting?"

"I really have to insist," Victor said conversationally. "Any cases, purses, and bags need a visual inspection. You know people can 3D print guns now? Plastic pieces. In their homes too; you believe that? Only good for one shot, but sometimes one is all you need."

"I don't mind," Sophie said, giving Greer a sparkling smile that she didn't feel. "Really, you worry too much. I supposed this might be policy in a place like this." With her free hand, she reached under the coat and withdrew the clutch, offering it to Victor. "Please, feel free."

The big man accepted it, and like a gorilla delicately opening a peanut, he popped the clasp and peeked inside. Reaching in, he raised an eyebrow and lifted out a string of mismatched beads and charms.

"A memento from a dear friend," Sophie said nostalgically.

With a respectful nod, Victor replaced the bracelet and closed the clutch with a snap, handing it back. "Thank you, Miss Quinn. Right this way."

Shooting a wink to a visibly dumbfounded Greer, Sophie returned the clutch to the hand under the jacket. Popping it open in one hand, muffled by her coat, she delicately dropped the pistol she held pinched between her concealed fingers back in.

Thank you, Ron Gavriel, Sophie thought to herself, rolling her skillful digits in satisfaction.

And then they were in.

The VIP room smelled like champagne and shoe polish. Dark violet carpets and bold green felt were framed with opulent mahogany furniture and a card table set with gold inlays. Panels of the same uniformly rumpled velvet they'd seen before covered the edges of the room, and the only breaks in the dark, sound-devouring walls were the door Victor was closing behind them and the red-and-white plastic of a fire alarm set into the wall, the offering to safety and normalcy catching Sophie's eye for a moment as she came to a stop.

Hidden speakers played music so clearly that for a moment, Sophie believed a string quartet might be concealed behind one of the velvet wall panels the same way the hidden entrance to this room had been. A dealer in a white button-down and black arm bands was accepting back cards from a table of lively men as varied as their commonplace counterparts on the dancefloor. White and black suits, cowboy hats, slicked back hair, designer jeans with designer holes ripped in designer locations, and one woman in a red dress that covered every inch between her wrists and ankles. The woman gave Sophie an appraising look as she entered and returned the slight nod that Sophie sent her way, more likely from politeness than from any secret understanding between the only two women in the room not serving drinks.

And at the center of the table, in a tailored suit held together with a diamond-studded tie clip and golden cuff-links, sat the vigorous Henry De Soto. Grey at the temples and a bit flabby around the waist, but with a vibrant color in his skin and a twitchy energy in his movements.

"Wow!" De Soto exclaimed, tossing his hands over his head. "Just—wow! It really is you. Look at that." Shooting to his feet, De Soto rushed to Sophie, offering a hand.

Unsure what was happening, Sophie took it, and De Soto clamped his other hand over it to create a handshake sandwich as he leaned in close and said. "Miss Sophie Quinn, I want you to know what an absolute honor and privilege it is to host you in my club. I loved," here De Soto tilted back and shot the word 'loved' toward the ceiling with the gusto of a man half his age, "and I mean lov-ed *Mysteries and Phenomena with Sophie Quinn.* My dear mother, rest her soul, and I used to watch it together. And she told me—you know what she used to tell me?"

Sophie's mouth opened in shock. She had come here prepared to fight for her life, and instead, the infamous Henry De Soto, Louisiana mobster and possibly the man who had ordered the killings of Maya Rossi and Josephine Ramsey, was gushing like-like—well, like Greer's daughter, Kinsley, had when they first met.

If De Soto noticed her stunned silence, he was polite enough to make no comment, continuing his breakneck recollections by lifting a finger. "She used to tell me if I was *half* as clever as that Sophie Quinn, I'd be running every city from here to Chicago. Now how do you like that? My own mother!" With a boisterous guffaw, De Soto turned to the table, conjuring a fresh wave of laughter from the assembled card sharks.

"So anyway," he continued. "When I heard you were in my club, I had to meet you. I had to know. Do you like cards, Miss Quinn?" De Soto asked, stepping toward the table and gesturing to one of a few empty seats.

Having gathered herself by the time she reached the table, Sophie put a hand on De Soto's shoulder, returning the man's amiable gestures. "Yes. Thank you, always a pleasure to meet a true fan. I love cards."

"Wonderful! And, erm, this... gentleman?" De Soto raised an eyebrow toward Greer.

Sophie gave a dismissive wave, not even fully looking the FBI agent's way. "My bodyguard. Don't mind him." And hopefully they wouldn't. Undercover or not, if any of the dangerous men in De Soto's VIP room recognized Greer, this unexpected hospitality could quickly and decisively fall through. "What are we playing?" Sophie prompted, hurrying the conversation along.

"Hold 'Em," replied the man in the cowboy hat. "Small blind is $500. Buy-in is a hundred grand. You ok with that, sweetie?"

Sophie tightened her stomach against an icy stab, keeping the placid smile on her face. Flashes of her bank balance in the hospital room returned like vengeful ghosts. Was she ok putting up a hundred-thousand-dollar buy-in? No. Oh Lord, no. Her days of throwing around that sort of cash were long gone. But now that she was here, what choice did she have?

De Soto. He was a fan. He might agree to put up her buy-in if she—

"Of course she is!" De Soto shouted, an edge of indignation in his voice. "This is Sophie Quinn. You wouldn't ask David Copperfield if he was good for it. You wouldn't ask... what's his name," De Soto snapped his fingers, as he wheeled his wrist, looking at Sophie as if she might have any idea who he's reaching for. "Big fella, works a stage show with a little mute,"

"Penn and Teller?" offered the man in the ripped jeans with a voice like a boot being pulled up from mud.

"That's the one," De Soto confirmed, jabbing a finger his way. "Now that's settled; let's play some cards."

The dealer motioned to one of the serving girls, and a moment later, on De Soto's emphatic word and the begrudging acceptance of the table, a pile of multicolored poker chips were slid Sophie's way. One by one, face-down cards slipped silently over the felt.

Sophie closed her eyes, taking a steadying breath. She tried not to think of her father's hospital bill, or the promised bribe to the man she hoped would give her the key to RK's connection to the MLM militia group.

Right now, losing her money was a secondary concern. Her priority was finding a killer. And for that, she was willing to lose her pound of flesh.

After all, the determined bleed for what they want.

Sophie picked up her cards.

Chapter 9

"Lettin' a goddamn magician play in a poker game." The man in the cowboy hat pounded the table as he stood, stomping away.

The game had been going for nearly two hours. The man in the white suit had gone out first. Robbie LeClaire, a loan shark and racketeer, but not the man she was looking for. Then the man in ripped jeans had gone all in. Jojo Bingham: oversees a fistful of pimps and manages meth distribution in-state. Also not a likely suspect in ordering the murders of Maya Rossi and Josephine Ramsey.

Sophie had been careful not to be too cavalier with her plays. She couldn't afford to lose big, couldn't afford to leave the table yet. And frankly, couldn't *afford* to lose. But one by one, she picked out the card sharks, relying on her own steel-trap memory and discrete glances to Greer to rule them out, to see if any man, apart from De Soto, might have a connection to their case. And then, with a look here, a blushing bluff there, she helped them leave the table.

Just as she'd helped Minster Brand, the cowboy counterfeiter and exotic animal smuggler, out of the game. Then again, she couldn't take all the credit. He had been excessively confident for a man holding a pair of nines.

If only she had a chance to shuffle. If she could deal the cards, this would be easy. But this wasn't a casual game. The dealer was De Soto's man, and that meant Sophie never touched the deck. For all her skill, she had no way to force herself a good hand. She had to rely on her ability to read people… and her own questionable luck.

There were a few moments, clutching her cards, letting practiced calm shield her expression, that Sophie seriously considered running for the fire alarm and trying to escape. If she didn't win or find a way out of this game, she would be on the hook for a hundred thousand dollars to De Soto. And as she suspected Jonathan Sharpe knew all too well, these were not men she wanted to owe.

Now there were only three. Sophie. De Soto. And Miriam Carter-Blanc, the woman in the red dress.

A woman that, from the blank looks her partner shot her, neither she nor Greer seemed to have any idea about, only piecing together her name from the other members of the table.

The dealer silently slipped out fresh hands.

Nine of spades. Queen of spades.

Good. But not a sure thing.

Sophie called the blind, tossing in her chips as the new hand began.

De Soto folded, sliding his cards to the center of the table. For all his enthusiasm, Sophie had quickly picked up that the older man had two speeds, full-stop or all-in. Oh, he tried to be clever, but the man was too timid when he wasn't sure of his hand, and too reckless when he w as.

The dealer turned the flop cards.

"Jack of spades. Ten of hearts. Ten of spades."

"Ten-thousand," the mysterious woman in the red dress said, her dark eyes locking with Sophie's.

Her stomach clenched. Another strong bet.

What did she have? Tens? If she was holding two tens, that would be four of a kind, a powerful hand to contend with. Sophie met the woman's gaze, their eyes intent on one another.

From what she could tell, the enigmatic Miriam Carter-Blanc had the same ideas about poker as Sophie. Play the players, not the game. She liked to stare, her dark eyes skewering people as if she were a teacher demanding an explanation for each play. And that hypnotic, cobra stare had a way of getting answers. Licking lips and flicking cards. Sudden stillness or the abrupt need to fidget with the end of their nose. Sophie had seen all the same tells she guessed Miriam had. Without absolute control, there were always tells.

Sophie ran through her mental checklist, taking a moment to adjust her body language, just as she'd done throughout the game. She knew her heart was racing too fast to be completely stoic, but if she kept adjusting her behavior, she might add enough conflicting information to keep the card shark confused.

But as for what Miriam was holding? The other woman's face may as well have been etched in glass. Sophie looked at her pile of chips, not quite half the formidable stack in front of the red-dressed woman. Maybe she was bluffing. Trying to force Sophie out?

"Call," Sophie said, sliding her chips into the center of the table. Whether this was what Miriam wanted or not, Sophie couldn't tell, but she watched the woman intently trying to locate a crack in her placid façade.

But Miriam only waited. Almost acting as though it was still Sophie's turn.

Or as if she were secretly coming to some decision.

"Miss Quinn," Miriam said tranquilly. "We've been having such fun. I have neglected to be a good conversationalist. Tell me, what have you been doing lately? Mr. De Soto has told us all how much he enjoys your shows, but you were canceled perhaps six years ago now, no?"

Sophie was momentarily taken aback. This was more than the other woman had said since she'd entered the room.

The dealer turned the next card. "Ace of clubs."

Miriam smiled. "Fifty thousand," she said demurely, letting the chips clack in her hands as she placed them in the center of the table, her gaze not leaving Sophie for a moment.

It took Sophie a moment to realize she was trying to distract her. And succeeding. Perhaps she wants to use her history to unnerve her?

Sophie thought of her own cards. Four spades, she nearly had a flush. She was also looking at a nine, ten, jack, and queen. Nearly a straight. If the stars aligned, maybe even a straight flush, just about an unbeatable han d... *if* the last card was in her favor.

In more practical terms, she was holding nothing...

But what was Miriam holding?

"I apologize," Miriam said with a light laugh. "You're trying to focus, and I'm distracting you. I just can't help but wonder, these years out of the spotlight. I've heard rumors that you have quite a chip on your shoulder after your sister's death."

Molly. Sophie felt a flash of pain in her heart, her lips drawing tight, the cards in her hand bending as her fingers stiffened.

"It's quite the story, I'm surprised you hadn't heard, Mr. De Soto," said Miriam. "Yes, Miss Quinn here was one of the victims of that massacre, the only one to escape. Now, what did they call him? The River Killer... yes, that was it."

The mobster was frowning now, his eyes narrowing as they darted between the two younger women at his table, but Sophie was only vaguely aware of the look. Her heart was racing. Her next breath came in a shudder as the man in ripped jeans lit a cigar.

There was no concealing her distress now, she could feel her pupils dilating. Her vision swam as the rumpled velvet on the walls appeared to roll like bayou water.

What's this now? growled a demonic voice at the back of Sophie's brain. A heavy Cajun accent like a dark reflection of her own, a voice she'd last heard the night her sister died. *Looks like you gotta fan, cher. Not for your tricky lil' fingers though, non... A fan of your sufferin?* The voice in her head, RK's voice, laughed at its own comment, merging with the light, mocking laugh coming from Miriam Carter-Blanc.

She was losing herself; Sophie felt her head spinning. Vaguely she was aware of her hands trying to sort her poker chips. Trying to call the bet. She bit the inside of her cheek, using the pain to focus and to pull herself back from the edge of the flashback threatening to swallow her.

"The River Killer," Miriam repeated. "He's why you gave up show business. Why you tried to join the FBI." The men in the room shuffled. Muffled curses and shifting furniture broke through the pounding blood in Sophie's ears as the woman said, "Why you're helping them right this second. A little tit for tat, eh?" Her dark eyes glanced to Greer, giving Sophie a knowing look.

Sophie locked her gaze with Miriam's, leaving her cards on the table, dread and confusion tumbling in her as she tried to pull the woman's face from any of the hundreds she'd poured over in her years of investigation. "Who are you?" Sophie asked.

"Just your bad luck, I guess," the woman in the red dress said with a shrug, standing up from the table as she did.

Then all hell broke loose.

A fire alarm screamed, flashing red and white light suddenly strobing over the room. Sophie's head spun to face where she'd seen the alarm.

Greer.

He let go of the plastic handle just as De Soto shouted, his words lost under the blare of the alarm, rocking back on his chair and pointing at Sophie.

Victor, the doorman, was charging for her like a murderous bull. Greer's elbow came up, catching the big man in the nose before his other hand slammed into his throat, leaving the brute doubled over on the floor.

Serving girls were screaming, rushing to the edge of the room and ducking behind couches and tables as the other guests each made their choice of fight or flight. Sophie hurried for Greer but froze as the door into the room flew open.

One of the men from the hall, the one who'd given Greer his pat-down, raised his submachine gun, leveling it at Greer with professional indifference to the chaos around him.

A muzzle flash, and the blast of a gunshot.

And the mob soldier fell back against the wall.

Sophie lowered her clutch, her concealed pistol now out in one trembling hand. Her eyes locked on the red running from high on the man's chest, just a few inches below his Adam's apple, a place no Kevlar vest would cover.

Greer dove for the man's submachine gun, hitting the ground just as the second guard entered the room. He barely had a moment to register the FBI agent lying on top of his dead coworker before Greer fired. A line of bullets danced up the second guard's leg, across his groin, and over his chest, and his own gun fired erratically into the wall as he fell with a scream.

"De Soto!"

Sophie saw more than heard Greer's shout. As she turned, looking around and through the huddled guests, she didn't see the mob boss. An icicle of panic stiffened her spine as if she'd been stabbed. They couldn't afford to lose him. Not now. Not after all of this. Stifling a curse, Sophie looked around the room for any sign of another exit. A distant part of her marked that she no longer saw Miriam either, but she dismissed it.

One catastrophe at a time.

There. One of the velvet wall panels was rippling, not being pulled like the ones the guests and serving girls were huddling beside. No, more like a draft.

Sophie rushed for it, pushing the panel the same way she'd seen Victor do when he let them through the secret passage to the VIP room. The wall opened into a concrete tunnel, a gap between the secret room and the building's exterior wall. It was dusty but clear, and bare bulbs lit the way to a steel door.

At the far end was De Soto, huffing as he ran pell-mell for the exit.

Kicking off her heels, Sophie threw on her jacket as she ran barefoot after the escaping mobster.

The fire alarm faded until all Sophie heard was the pounding in her ears. De Soto was out. The steel door was on the edge of closing; beyond was the shallow darkness of a starlit alleyway, the scent of wet concrete. Sophie lowered her shoulder, driving into the door with reckless abandon.

It opened barely a foot before the steel came to a sudden, jarring stop.

Sophie's shoulder screamed. She felt something pop in the joint, and if it had been the arm holding her pistol, she was sure she would have dropped it. She let out a fierce grunt, and as the door rebounded, Sophie lifted her bare heel, kicking it open again. This time it opened wide enough for Sophie to quickly rush through.

Lying on the ground in front of her, both hands clutching the back of his head where the edge of the door had cracked his skull, lay Henry De Soto.

The snarl twisting his lips disappeared as Sophie raised her pistol.

"Alright, Henry. I have some questions for my biggest fan."

Chapter 10

"What are you trying to do? Intimidate me?" Henry De Soto scoffed, twisting to spit into the moonlit canal behind him. Overhead, the bridge to the highway flashed with occasional headlights, but nothing that reached them down by the water's edge, down with the mud fish and the snakes. "I've had better guns in my face than that princess piece you're carrying, sweetheart. And even then, I don't talk. So why don't you walk away before this gets any worse for you, huh?"

Sophie rolled her shoulder, still trying to work the stiffness out from where she'd dislocated it ramming De Soto's back door. Once they'd had De Soto cuffed in the back of Greer's Interceptor, he'd taken a moment to pop it back into place for her, but it would still be a few minutes before the aspirin took effect.

"Josephine Ramsey. Maya Rossi." Greer folded his arms, taking a step forward, crowding the mob boss. But De Soto didn't back up, so an inch away from his face, Greer barked. "Two women are dead, De Soto. Talk."

"Cry me a river," De Soto mocked. "We both know you're FBI and that means you have rules. This is all foreplay, but we know the real action is when you give up, take me to the station, and get me a coffee while we wait for my lawyer." He turned to Sophie, "Two sugars, no cream. Write it down if you have to."

It didn't surprise Sophie that this was what De Soto thought should happen, what he thought *would* happen. He'd clam up, wait for his mob lawyer, and they'd be back to square one.

But that was why they weren't at the field office.

"You seem really sure that we're FBI," Sophie said stepping forward as Greer stepped back.

De Soto rolled his eyes. "Please, he's got it written all over him. Bodyguard. Shame on me, I should have known better. Should have known better about you too. Sophie Quinn, bureau bitch."

"What, I'm FBI just because Miriam says so?" Sophie asked. She tilted her head, letting the question dangle for a moment. "We didn't show up wearing badges and wires. We came with guns." Sophie let her voice drop, going quieter, drawing De Soto in so that he had to strain to hear. "We killed your men." It had been self-defense, but she didn't need to belabor *that* point. "This might all be theater. Then again, how many bodies do you think have ended up in this canal over the years?"

De Soto swallowed, and the scant moonlight caught beads of sweat beginning to spread on his forehead and cheeks. Not the hot sweat of their chase, a cold sweat. Fear. Sophie could smell it.

"Miriam was wrong about some things," Sophie lied. "But she was right about one part—" Sophie's hand shot forward, and she grabbed De Soto by his flabby cheeks, pinching them together in a vice grip around his jaw. "I do have a chip on my shoulder. And if there's a line I won't cross to get what I need, I haven't found it yet."

She let the chill air of the summer night seep into her veins, giving her stare an icy quality as De Soto squirmed and jerked his head free of her grasp.

"You may want to answer the questions now," Greer said.

De Soto's eyes flared. He was trembling now. Sophie could tell she was getting to him. But there was still something there. Pride maybe? He wasn't broken... not yet.

"Big mistake," De Soto growled. "On account of how happy your shows made my mother, I was prepared to let this go. Just a bad call on your part, nothing unforgivable. But now?" De Soto stomped forward, throwing his sizable stomach towards Sophie and physically pushing her back when she refused to retreat. "Now I'm coming for you, Sophie Quinn. Sleep with the lights on. Call your loved ones and tell them to lock the doors at night. Hide your pets. Because now, now you've really *pissed me off.*" Even cuffed, he tromped forward until Greer grabbed him by his shoulders to physically hold him back.

Fear had given way to anger. And that anger gave way to threats, the only tool left in his arsenal. Sophie grinned. He was at the tipping point.

She raised her chin, pacing around De Soto until the moonlight carved a Halloween mask of shadow on her features. She threw her eyes wide, letting the whites show in an overt display of insane focus, a look she'd cultivated for spook shows and guest star appearances in horror programs. She was a performer, her body and expressions a weapon for her to wield. "I've already lost my sister to a killer," Sophie said darkly. "I've been beaten, strangled, drowned... You're threatening a dead woman."

While Greer held De Soto in place, Sophie reached into her jacket and drew out one of her lockpicks from the black leather case, selecting a heavy, wide-tongued piece. It was dull, but the wide blade of the pick could easily be mistaken for a knife in the gloom.

"I want answers," Sophie continued. She grabbed De Soto's wrist, pulling his hand forward and twisting one finger up and away from the others. "Maybe if I get them, we can all leave happy and with all our fingers? Hmm? For you, I might even throw in an autograph. How did you put it?" Sophie tapped the dull blade to her lips. "I'm prepared to let this go. Nothing unforgivable; just a bad call on your part." Sophie menacingly lowered the metal blade of the pick.

"You're crazy!" De Soto shouted, squirming, trying to pull his cuffed hands free as Greer implacably held him in place.

"Come on now, Henry," Sophie prompted, adding a lilt of deranged cheerfulness to her voice. "Remember what your mother used to say? Be clever now, Henry."

Sophie could see the struggle on his face as he seemed to consider screaming for help, not that anyone would hear him or that any of the drivers passing on the bridge would catch his words at high speed. But even if someone had been around to hear, Sophie didn't think he would shout. Henry De Soto knew what *he* would do if their positions were reversed and she tried calling for help... and now he believed Sophie and Greer were capable of the same sorts of actions.

He was broken.

"Alright! Alright!" De Soto squealed, his voice drowning in panic. "You win. I'm talking. I'm talking, just put that knife down!"

Sophie obliged, stepping back and tucking away the fake blade. "James Rossi," Sophie started. "He had a wife Maya Rossi."

De Soto squinted, blinking quickly as sweat rolled into the corners of his eyes. "I don't know any Rossis," he said hesitantly.

From over his shoulder, Greer rumbled, "James had a fight a few weeks back at the Black Coral Club. He was thrown out. Then his wife was found murdered."

"So?" De Soto looked genuinely confused, then he hurriedly added, "We get fights at the club all the time. You put enough people in a room and someone is going to get punched. We don't send button men to deal with every drunken brawl."

"There was nothing particular about Rossi's fight?" Sophie asked. "Nothing to make an example out of? A police report was filed but no charges were laid."

"Police?" De Soto lowered his chin, his eyes scanning the wet ground for the answers. "Wait—that asshole?" With a frustrated sigh, the mobster shook his head. "I remember now. Victor took care of it. He got into it with some other guys, I guess his brother-in-law and some friends? But he hung around after, tried to get the police involved. Like I said, Victor took care of it. We have an understanding with the cops; people getting arrested outside the club—it's bad for business. Look, Victor made sure he knew he wasn't *welcome* anymore, but we're not going to grease the guy for that."

Sophie rubbed her tongue along the inside of her teeth thoughtfully. If that was true, then De Soto and his mobsters wouldn't have a connection to Maya Rossi's death. And she no longer had a convenient reason to believe James Rossi's confession wasn't the truth.

Meeting Greer's eye, she could see the same thoughts churning in his head. He mouthed 'truth' to her and Sophie nodded. De Soto was past the point of trying to strong-arm a lie through. What he'd said was near enough to the truth not to raise any red flags. And Sophie had spent two hours playing poker with the man... she had a pretty good grasp of his 'tells'.

"What about Josephine Ramsey?" Sophie asked. "Her husband Jonathan—"

"I remember Jonny Sharpe," De Soto bowled over Sophie's question. "He played at my tables. Funny guy. Not too good at cards. Wait..." Something seemed to suddenly click for the mobster. "Did someone take out Jo Ramsey?"

Sophie raised an eyebrow. "Josephine Ramsey? Yes, she was found dead this morning."

He clicked his tongue, wagging his head like he'd just heard Christmas was canceled. "That's a shame. She was a treasure. That husband of hers had got himself in debt. That's why you're talking to me, isn't it?"

Sophie confirmed the suspicion with a subtle nod, trying to take in the big man's body language. Disappointment but also... relief? He thinks he's off the hook, Sophie thought to herself.

"Jo Ramsey called me one day. She knew Jonny's debts were getting out of hand. She also knew having a couple leg-breakers show up at her house could put her law career in jeopardy. So, gem of a woman that she was, she took care of it. We made a deal. She cleared the debt, with interest, and I don't let Jonny sit at the table anymore."

"So you have nothing against Jonathan Sharpe?" Greer asked, the skepticism clear in his voice.

"Nothing. We're square. And I certainly had nothing against his wife. Look, playing hard ball is part of the game, but at the end of the day, I'm a business man; I'd much rather have the money. I can't exactly buy a new car with fingers and broken kneecaps, can I?"

"Any proof?" Sophie asked. She couldn't totally rule out the possibility that—despite his performance at the poker table—Henry De Soto may be an extraordinary liar.

"Yeah," he replied bluntly. "If you get my phone, I can show you texts from Jo. And if that doesn't do it, I can show you where she wired me the money."

Over the next five minutes, he did just that.

The trio gave each other appraising looks as Greer took back his cuffs and De Soto rubbed the circulation back into his wrists.

"We can give you a ride back to the club," Sophie offered, keeping her tone professional and cool. She wanted to be diplomatic, not apologetic. After all, certain threats had been made both ways.

"That's it?" De Soto said, almost sounding insulted. "We drive back. You go your way, I go mine. We both just forget the whole thing?"

It did sound slightly ridiculous when he put it that way. But what was the alternative? Leave him in the ditch or hope he's too busy for revenge? Then again, as De Soto had said, sometimes hard ball is just a part of doing business.

Holding up a finger. Sophie reached into her jacket, withdrawing her deck of cards and a thick black marker as she whistled to Greer. With some confusion, he followed her direction and turned around while Sophie used his back to sign the playing card.

"Ace of hearts, signed by Sophie Quinn," she said, extending the card like a borrowed lighter, friendly and grateful.

De Soto took the offered card, his perplexed expression cracking into a grin as he tapped it against his fingers. "You really are crazy, you know that?"

Sophie shrugged noncommittally. Maybe she was.

With a disbelieving shake of his head, De Soto said, "We're not even." Then, meeting her eyes, he added, "But we're close enough. I'd accept the ride, but it's probably best you not show your faces at the club." He offered a hand and Sophie took it. "Thanks for the memorable night, Miss Quinn. It was... invigorating."

De Soto started walking up the canalway, his phone going to his ear. Sophie presumed he was calling for a ride... or to order a hit on her. She supposed time would tell.

As Greer shut the door to the white sedan, he and Sophie simply sat in silence for a moment. He didn't look at her. As his blue eyes stared off through the windshield, Sophie shifted uncomfortably in her seat.

She thought back to the moment at the bar. When he'd stroked her hand, the look they'd shared. There was something there, wasn't there? She hadn't imagined it.

"You've done that before?" Greer said. His voice was flat, restrained. Only the silence that stretched afterward told Sophie it had been a question.

She nodded.

"You said we'd stop; see if we could get him to talk before he lawyers up. Next thing I know, we're talking about taking fingers?" Greer shook his head. "There are reasons we're not allowed to just do whatever we want."

"I wasn't actually going to hurt him," Sophie said quietly. "It wasn't even a real knife."

"That's not the point," Greer said wearily.

"Isn't it?" Sophie turned in the passenger seat. "We got the info we needed. We cleared De Soto and his club. I didn't actually hurt him. Just scared him. It's just a character I can play."

Greer shifted in his seat, his gaze meeting Sophie's. The lines around his eyes, his mouth. There was a tortured sort of pity in that look, and his breath shuddered slightly as he said, "It's a character. Now. You put on a mask, and it lets you do things you'd never do. You tell yourself it's just a mask. It's not the real you. But then one day, the mask won't come off. And then you realize, the face on the mask... that's the real yo u."

Sophie blinked. Her eyes were tired, and she could feel the hot promise of what could be tears behind them. "Are you scared of me?" she asked softly.

"No," Greer replied. "I'm scared of your mask."

Chapter 11

"Break a bottle, and it's a nuisance. Break a cathedral window, and it's a tragedy. If two people ever deserved true happiness, it might be you. That's where the beauty of it comes from."

The Mask reached over the young man's shoulder and lit the elegant candelabra in front of him. His hand and arm wrapped in the midnight black of his ensemble, he moved the long-stemmed match to the final candle, completing the effect. A trio of warm lights coiled together and rose up like a spiral stair.

Stepping back, the Mask tilted his head, appreciating the artistry in the arrangement. Rose petals formed a path between the apartment's hallway door and the living room. Candlelight now. Behind the bone-white porcelain of his weeping mask, he smiled.

"A pair of star-cross'd lovers. You defied the odds. Secret rendezvous. She, cast out from her family home. And you, ready to run away with her. Setting up this little 'love nest'." The Mask gestured around the cramped one-bedroom apartment, nearly striking the wall behind him. "I can't say I approve, but you normally dine at the couch don't you?" He tutted. "Well, this will be a good change of pace for the both of you, I think."

The oven timer dinged, and the Mask rumpled the young man's thick, curly hair playfully. "That'll be the duck."

The young man weakly twisted in his chair, and a groan of protest came out, muffled by the gag stuffed and bound in his mouth. He struggled against the bindings on his wrists holding him to his seat.

"Ah, yes. Thank you for reminding me." As the Mask briskly stepped to the kitchen, he pressed play on the cheap stereo resting on the couple's living room shelves. "Silence would be extremely appropriate, and dramatic, but then I'd have to knock you out, and frankly, that's worse than a bit of atmospheric music. Don't you agree?"

The young man let out a groggy attempt at a shout, again drowned by his gag and the classical music now filling the space. "Yes, I knew you'd understand. It would be no good spoiling the climax before she can see you."

The apartment was damnably close. Almost suffocating. The Mask frowned as he again assessed the eye line between the front door and the living room. He had been able to pull a card table into the space between the kitchen and living room to form a sort of improvised dining room, and it was hardly ideal, but it did mean the young man's lady-love would need to fully enter the apartment before she could see her one-and-only at the table.

That did leave the question of where *he* would stand.

A loud *thud* and clatter rang from the table and the Mask rushed over.

The young man had somehow rocked his chair to the tipping point and fallen on the ground, though, he was still tied to it, thankfully.

"There, there," the Mask consoled him, patting the young man's toned arms as he carefully righted the chair. "That's no good now, is it? I know you were raised on romantic comedies, but that's not the story you're in. Those insipid things are a modern invention. Happily-ever-after, a disease that companies helmed by cartoon mice try to infect us with. Selling our destiny, the true weight of our existence for a quick buck."

Taking a length of cord from the counter behind him, the Mask wrapped a noose around the young man's throat, tightening it before tying the loose end to the slats in the chair back. Now any attempts at rocking would produce a sharp jerk on his neck. "You really should try to enjoy this. Your story will rise above the others around you. A true tragedy worthy of remark."

Stepping away, the Mask took the clean glass he'd selected earlier, well the cleanest he could find anyway, and began to pour the wine. Shaking his head, he recalled how he'd had to bring his own wine this time. "You really should keep something other than beer at hand. A broad palate is the mark of a cultured man, after all."

Setting the glass on a small end table near the apartment entrance, the Mask scattered a few rose petals around it. Yes, this really had been easier than he'd expected. So many lives on the edge of greatness; stories on the cusp of tragedy, only requiring a small *push* to elevate them.

From his back pocket, the Mask withdrew a thin book. He opened it one last time, taking a deep breath, inhaling the aroma of the old paper. He walked to the living room and settled the book on the coffee table. A bit on the nose, he acknowledged, but it would have to do. One should always honor their forebearers.

Hearing the rattle of a key in the lock, the Mask grinned and stepped into the hallway closet, reaching for the panel in the back and pulling the fuse switch. Through the door slats, he watched as the apartment fell into darkness, with only the waving glow of the candles around the corner.

As she stepped in, he could not help but whisper breathlessly within his mask, "For never was a story of more woe, than this of Juliet and her Romeo."

Chapter 12

I know your probably bzy. Or maybe you forgot. Dr has idea about y hes still comatoes. Something about brain pressure. I don't understand. Surgery day after tomorrow. It's ok. I'll stay with him tonight. ttyl. Mama.

She wasn't sure if her mother had signed the text message because she was from an older generation, or if she thought Sophie wouldn't have her number in her phone anymore. That was the thought that made Sophie pause as she blinked back tears.

She'd been sitting in her car outside her motel room for nearly half an hour, the cicada clicks and street light hum underscoring her silence like a desolate lullaby. The message had come sometime while she and Greer were still haranguing De Soto for any leads, and she hadn't noticed it until her partner had dropped her off at her car. Neither had said much on that final drive. Murmured goodnights and a brief confirmation that they'd check in again tomorrow at seven.

Below the message, Sophie had sent a 'thumbs up'. A compromise between spending any more time worrying about what to say—whether she should apologize and how—and not replying at all. She supposed the clipped message implied her father's condition hadn't changed. And she also supposed she could take that as a blessing. Maybe his body just needed more time. Once he'd recovered, once his mind was ready, he'd wake up. Any other possibility was a waste of time to consider.

In the dark of the driver's seat, Sophie anxiously twisted her bracelet between her fingers, turning over each bead, remembering the shape and color by touch alone. A sunflower from Barcelona. A painted beetle from Mexico. A little blues singer from Chicago. Over the years, Ron Gavriel's gifts had filled it until she'd been forced to restring them all on a longer thread. But she couldn't bear to hide away the old magician's gifts in a drawer somewhere.

Sophie glanced at her motel door. She knew she should sleep. But her mind was still too active. Thoughts were colliding against each other, fighting for her attention like piranha swarming for a scrap of food.

The worry about her father subsiding, fresh anxiety arrived in the form of the murder investigation. A mob boss could have made James Rossi and Jonny Sharpe confess to murders they didn't do. De Soto's involvement would have explained everything. Who else could do that? There was no other connection between the victims or their husbands that she or Greer could find.

At the thought of her partner, Sophie winced. She remembered the concern in those sky blues as they looked at her. It was almost like he hadn't recognized her at all. Sophie's stomach twisted, and she coiled the bracelet tight between her fingers, letting out a groan as she squeezed her eyes shut and tried to dismiss the image in her mind. But instead, all she could feel was the remembered sensation of the compassionate agent's hand on hers.

He had trusted her. Gone with her into the lion's den. Would he still trust her after this? Jonathan Greer had lines. With his family, his moral code... And it seemed all Sophie did was find new ways to cross them.

The echo of Dr. Walsh's mild flirtations in the autopsy room flashed in her mind. Greer's words at the bar overlapped the mental image, 'If someone did come along, I'd just keep an open mind.' Sophie felt sick but shook her head. This stupid crush was getting out of hand. She had work to do. She was still tracking RK, waiting for her contact to say when and where she should send his money. She was *still* on a murder investigation. She had too much to do to worry about catching feelings.

In that moment, she remembered the woman at the card table. Miriam Carter-Blanc. Who was she? Why did she know so much about what Sophie was doing back in Louisiana?

The sick feeling in her stomach hardened to a cold, iron ball as Sophie's shoulders hunched together. She leaned her forehead on the steering wheel. It was all getting to be too much. She needed some perspective.

Without thinking long enough to stop herself, Sophie scrolled through her contacts, listening to the ringing as she lifted the phone to her ear.

"Soph? That you?" A gruff, older voice answered, the words scraggly, as if he were simultaneously clearing his throat as he spoke.

"Hi, Ron. I hope I didn't wake you up."

"Wake me up?" the old hypnotist laughed. "It's only—" Sophie heard the shift and jangle of the loose wrist watch on Ron Gavriel's arm as he twisted to look at it. "Ok, it's almost midnight, but still. This ain't late for us."

Sophie couldn't help but let out a small chuckle. "No, I suppose it's not. Where are you, Ron? Still in Ft. Lauderdale?"

"Nah," Ron's high, Bostonian accent slipped in over his graveled voice. "That was only a one-night gig. I'm back in Atlanta for a two-week stint."

"They haven't kicked you out of there yet?"

Gavriel let out a single explosive snort. "Not under the name 'Gavriel' they ain't."

They shared a moment of amused chuckles, but only a moment. The line quieted for a heartbeat. Then two.

"Hey, kid. Is everything alright?" Ron asked, his voice coming down from its usual boisterous volume. "Not that I don't enjoy the pleasure of your company, but, eh, we're more pen-pals these days, y'know? So call me suspicious, but if Sophie Quinn's calling me up in the witching h our..."

"What, I can't just call up my former teacher just for old time's sake?" Sophie replied lamely.

Ron didn't reply, and as Sophie let out a sigh, she leaned back in her seat. "Ron, am I a good person?"

Softly, his rough voice blunted, Ron asked, "What's this about, Soph?"

Sophie rubbed her forehead, closing her eyes. "I'm on a case... and tonight, I had to do something. Nothing bad... nothing I haven't done before with other suspects... less-than-cooperative witnesses, you might call 'em. But tonight, I had Greer with me."

"The beanstalk?" Ron asked. "Same guy that brought me in the last case you were on?"

"Yeah," Sophie said. "I guess... No, not a guess. He told me. I freaked him out. Scared him."

"To be fair, you can be pretty intimidating when you want, kid," Ron said delicately.

"I know, but it's an act... right? I'm not really like that. I swear, the way he looked at me..." Sophie's heel was bouncing, her hand flexing and gesturing to Ron across the phoneline. "I'm not the bad guy. I just do whatever I can to put the bad guys away. I'm not a monster, I'm determined."

"Did he call you a monster?" Ron asked.

Sophie let out a long breath, shaking her head. "No. Not to my face. He just said something about masks." Of course, with Sophie's steel-trap memory, it only took a moment for her to look back and remember exactly what Greer had said. "He said, 'you put on a mask, and it lets you do things you'd never do. You tell yourself it's just a mask. It's not the real you. But then one day, the mask won't come off.' So, I guess—" The edge of her voice frayed, and Sophie could feel the exhaustion coming out in her words. "I guess what I'm saying is that I really want someone to tell me I'm *not* a bad person."

The way her mother looked at her, talked to her; the stress of her father's hospitalization; Greer; all of it. She'd been pushed to her limit. Faced with death day after day for weeks now, and all that after years of scraping and hunting for any whiff of the River Killer.

She'd told herself over and over, the determined bleed for what they want; the obsessed make everyone else bleed. If she was the only one suffering, it must be determination. But was that true still?

Gavriel's phone crackled as he, wherever he was, shifted position. When he spoke again, his voice was warm and slow like a parent talking to their child. "Look kid, I'm just an old hypnotist. I don't have the answers to life's mysteries. You've known me long enough to know, I'm out here figuring it out, the same as anyone else. But the way I see it... Good person. Bad person. You're a person, Soph. A person, just like the rest of us. And instead of trying to figure out whether your moral compass points true north or not, maybe just figure out where it's trying to take you? Does that make sense?"

Letting out a small sniff, Sophie rubbed the corner of her eye and let out a single, mirthless laugh. "No, Ron. Not really."

Ron gave back a gentle chuckle of his own. "I guess all I'm saying is: you have something so important that to you it's worth everything. It's worth dying for even. Something that'll make other people around you uncomfortable because they don't see it the way you do. Right, wrong, or otherwise."

Something worth dying for. Sophie's father had been shot trying to intervene in a fight between his neighbors, trying to keep the peace. She thought again about her parents' refusal to let her move them out of Peillon. Why had they stayed? Their community. Friends and family gathered around the crawdad boil? Was it that simple? To them, this imperfect, dangerous place... was it worth dying for?

"You there, Soph? Hello?" *BEEP BEEP* the phone chirped and blared in Sophie's ear as Ron pressed the buttons of his phone from his side.

"I'm here. Ron, I'm here! You didn't get disconnected."

"Oh, good. Did you hear what I—?"

"Yes." Sophie put a hand over her face. "Thank you, Ron. I appreciate you answering."

"Forget about it, kid," the old magician replied warmly. "Get some rest now. Sounds like you need it."

She did. And for a few hours, Sophie slept like the dead. She likely would have slept on longer, if not for the call that dragged her back to consciousness in her motel bed.

"Greer?"

"Miss Quinn," Jonathan Greer replied professionally, the curt tone cutting her more than Sophie expected.

"What is it?"

"Merchant just called me. There's a new victim."

Chapter 13

"The neighbors said the smoke alarm was going off," Greer explained, handing Sophie a cup of coffee that still retained most of its original heat. "No one answered the door, so they called the fire department. They realized after they called that it was unlocked."

A flash lit up the small apartment as the crime scene technician took another photograph. Another splash of unforgiving light on the figure seated at a licorice black card table, plastic plates cramped around stuffed potatoes, peppered asparagus, and a roast duck glistening in its own congealed grease.

The sounds of Baton Rouge's rush hour traffic outside, honking horns and indistinct shouts, felt almost profane against the image of the pretty young woman propped in the chair in front of her. Her luscious, raven hair fell back nearly to the floor, so dark that it hid the stain of the blood from her slit throat.

"God, she looks like a kid," Sophie murmured.

"Eden Garza, nineteen," Greer replied. "She shares the apartment with her boyfriend, Marcus Baker. He's still missing."

"Just like the others were," Sophie said.

"Just like the others," Greer confirmed solemnly.

Sophie took in the scene as best she could. The local police had a detective and two support officers on scene. They had kicked out the local crime scene tech when the FBI's technician arrived. And now that Sophie and Greer were here, that was six people sharing a space that was tight for even two.

Seven, Sophie thought, correcting herself as she examined Eden Garza's arms.

"We have bruising," she said. "She was tied up like the others. Looks more severe, though." Sophie chewed her lip a moment, looking down to a wine stain on the carpet beside her, a toppled drinking glass upended over it. "She may have been attacked more quickly. Tied up before the drugs took effect."

"Or she didn't drink it at all," Greer offered. "If she was struggling that badly."

It was a thought, a potential difference. With serial killers, the ritual was so important, though. Was the drugged wine just a tool? Or was it significant to the killer's obsession?

This close to the kitchen, Sophie could smell the acrid, burnt toast scent coming from the open oven. "Was that still on when the fire department arrived?" she asked Greer.

He nodded. "They think that's what set off the smoke alarm. Whoever last used it, must have forgotten to turn it off when they left. We're checking it for prints, but if it's like the last two scenes, the killer was likely wearing gloves."

Turning to face the living room, Sophie finally took a drink of the coffee Greer had given her. One cream, no sweetener. Perfect. Had he remembered? Sophie glanced at her partner. He looked as exhausted as she felt, his face a stubbled piece of marble as he sipped his own coffee.

"Thanks," Sophie said, raising her cup to Greer.

He shook his chin subtly, his steel blue eyes not straying from the scene around them. "Don't mention it."

His body language was stiff. Reserved. Sophie remembered the first time she'd ridden in a car with the former Marine, after she'd tricked him into thinking she was the coroner. That same straight-backed, 'everything-is-fine' posture was back. The wall was up again.

Sophie tried to think what to say, what she could do. This wasn't good. They needed to be a team if nothing else. If she took Merchant's offer to stay down here, to move to the Louisiana field office, she would need all the allies she could get. And more than that... she *liked* Greer. He was a good man, strong but compassionate. Nothing stings quite like the disapproval of someone you admire.

The crime scene tech's camera flashed again, pulling Sophie out of her reverie. She wandered away from Greer, trying to put some space between them while examining the living room.

There was a cheap stereo tagged with an evidence flag. A well-loved couch with sagging seats. A coffee table—

Sophie frowned, freezing in place. She glanced around the room. Shelves with video games, shot glasses, football memorabilia. She looked back to the coffee table, crouching down beside it.

"What is it?" Greer was beside her, his eyebrow furrowing as he craned his neck to follow her gaze.

Putting on a pair of disposable gloves, Sophie tapped the thin book resting in the center of the coffee table. "This doesn't belong," she said simply.

Greer read the title over her shoulder as Sophie picked up the sliver of a book. "*The Most Excellent and Lamentable Tragedy of Romeo and Juliet*. Wait, this is the play, right? Shakespeare. Every high schooler has to read it at some point. What's it doing here?"

Sophie opened the playbook, flipping over the first few pages. "No library stamp. No name or class number. It doesn't look like a holdover from high school."

"Maybe one of them had a soft spot for Shakespeare. It's not the weirdest thing I've heard," Greer said, though, he sounded unconvinced. "Or a gift?"

"Maybe," Sophie said. "But look around." She stood, gesturing to the living room shelves, then crossed to a sparse bedroom that, while messy, contained only a rumpled bed, a cracked hamper, and a particle board dresser. "No bookshelves. No e-readers or loose books and plays anywhere. Why is this here?" Sophie shook the playbook, flipping through the pages for any highlighted lines or underlining to show it had been used. But there was nothing. "It's possible one of them had a specific connection to *Romeo & Juliet*, and *only* that play, but it feels odd."

And then it hit her, why it stood out.

"It's them," Sophie said faintly. "The killer saw them as Romeo and Juliet, two young lovers trying to make it on their own. He saw the story, then came to finish it."

Greer held up a palm, sweeping his coffee in slow gestures like he was gathering his thoughts by hand. "Hold on. What about the other victims? Yes, they're all couples, but Ramsey was in her forties. Maya Rossi was in her late-twenties. And they'd each been married for years. That doesn't exactly fit Romeo & Juliet."

"Pull up the crime scenes," Sophie said. "If this is him, it's not the only story he'll lean on." She was pacing now, setting down her own coffee as she tapped the book in her open hand. "He'll have other stories he wants to tell. This is the ritual. So that means he'll have left other books. We didn't know to look for them, so they might not have stood out before."

As Greer hurriedly pulled up the crime scene photos, Sophie took a deep breath. She had to look back. Something was there. Something she'd seen but didn't realize. Closing her eyes, Sophie paused in her pacing. She needed to open her mind, to let the knowledge float to the surface. She inhaled; slow, exaggerated, filling her lungs; and put a hand to her grey suit-coat, feeling the inner pocket over her heart.

Inside, a brass pocketwatch ticked away. Her heart was racing, the adrenaline of discovery pushing her. But she didn't need adrenaline. She needed calm. She felt the pulse of her heartbeat clash with the pocketwatch. Then it began to slow, to fall into rhythm. She let her perceptions drift, to follow the currents of her intentions.

She was back in the home of Josephine Ramsey. She looked down at the spilled couscous, the broken wine glass; Greer was there, by the door. She stepped away from the table, circling it. Curtains were drawn on a bay window facing the street.

A bay window with little shelves built in. Books. Leatherbound classics.

One by one, the titles slipped by in her mind's eye.

Treasure Island... Don Quixote...

...

The Tragedie of Antony and Cleopatra

Sophie's eyes flew open with a sudden sharp inhalation.

"*Antony & Cleopatra*," she said abruptly. "At the Ramsey crime scene."

Greer quickly turned his phone to face Sophie. "There was a side table in the Rossi house. We took a picture because it was where she set the wine glass. I just thought it was one of those table books, you know, the sort you put out for decoration."

Slightly out of focus in the picture and obscured by the wine glass in the foreground lay a heavy, green book. It was difficult to make out, but as Greer slid a finger across the screen, the image zoomed in.

"*The Iliad*," Sophie said.

"That's not Shakespeare," Greer noted uncertainly.

"No, but it's a connection." Sophie motioned for a forensics tech. "Bag this," she ordered. "We need to check it for prints and DNA." As the tech retreated, she pulled off her gloves with an enthusiastic snap.

An image of the killer's motives—the nature of his ritual—was forming.

"Ok," Greer took another sip, closing his eyes as if he was listening to a complicated piece of music. "Explain it to me. What are you seeing?"

"He's mimicking the tragedies," Sophie quickly replied. "De Soto told us James Rossi was fighting with his brother-in-law at the club. It sounds like there's bad blood there. I bet if we follow up on that, someone sees Maya's marriage as James stealing her away from her family. *The Iliad—*" Sophie gestured to the image on Greer's phone, "is about the Trojan War. It starts when Paris of Troy elopes with Helen, you know, the infamous 'Helen of Troy', and sparks a war with her family, who come to reclaim her. James and Maya Rossi are Paris and Helen of Troy." From across the apartment, Sophie shot a finger toward the most recent victim. "Marcus Baker and Eden Garza are Romeo and Juliet. And do you remember what I told you Sharpe's sister said about him and his wife?"

"They referred to themselves as a 'king and queen'?" Greer said, his eyes widening as he caught up with Sophie's rapid-fire explanation.

"Exactly. They were the original power couple. Wealthy. Influential. On the shelf behind Ramsey's body was a copy of *Antony & Cleopatra*."

"So the killer's finding couples and giving them a tragic ending." Greer ran a hand over his stubbled chin thoughtfully. "But how's he convincing the men to confess?"

Sophie let out an explosive sigh, crossing her arms. It was a question that still bothered her too. Why not kill them both? Why make the men confess? And *how?*

Suddenly the detective and local cops across the room squawked, rushing to the apartment door. Sophie didn't catch what they were saying, only the urgent tone as she and Greer hurried to follow. "What is it?" she shouted after them.

Before she could receive an answer, she heard Greer behind her, answering his phone. With a curse, he hung up and ran for the door, Sophie hot on his heels.

“What’s going on?” she demanded.

“We found the boyfriend,” Greer shot back.

“So soon? Did he confess like the others?”

“I don’t know,” Greer huffed, making his way to the apartment steps. “But we have to get to him quick. He’s in a standoff with the police. And he’s got a gun.”

Chapter 14

Someone is going to die.

This was the first thought Sophie had as Greer parked in front of the urban mechanic shop. The red and blue of the cop cars' lights washed out in the morning sun, except where shadows pooled past the shop's blinded windows and the view slots cut in the garage doors. Baker Tire and Repair looked closed and if not for the fresh oil and relatively clean windows it might have even looked abandoned, so an outside observer might be forgiven if it looked to them like the Baton Rouge Police Department had only cornered a ghost.

Officers were redirecting traffic at the street's ends; setting up barricades. Behind a police van, Sophie caught sight of a middle-aged man in police blue, with the chevrons of a sergeant on his shoulder, giving orders through a radio.

"Street's closed, ma'am," the sergeant said, throwing a look to a nearby officer and gesturing for him to show Sophie and Greer away.

"We're FBI," Sophie said quickly as Greer held up his ID. "We need to get in there. That man is a witness in a murder investigation."

"Funny way to say he's a killer," the sergeant muttered back, turning his head to snap off an order before locking eyes with Sophie. "Marcus Baker, right?"

"That's right," Greer confirmed. "We just came from his apartment."

"Ok, yeah, that's our man. I'm Sergeant Jackson, Baton Rouge PD." As the trio exchanged a couple perfunctory handshakes, the sergeant said, "Baker's uncle owns this shop. It's closed, but we can't confirm if there's anyone in there with him. There have been several domestic disturbance reports involving Baker over the last year. He's been arrested before for taking a swing at his old man and pulling a gun on his uncle. We're trying to reach his family right now, but we just don't know who or how many people he's got in there with him. What we *do* know is he's got a gun and he's already taken a few shots when officers tried to approach. So nobody's approaching, got it?"

Sophie gritted her teeth. The story made perfect sense given what she knew. She'd bet that Baker's fights with his family had something to do with his girlfriend. This would play right into the real killer's Romeo and Juliet fantasy. But the details could be fleshed out later. What was important right now was talking to Baker. Why hadn't he gone to the police station and confessed like the others?

"I have to go in anyway. I can talk him down, I'm sure," Sophie said urgently.

"No can do," Sergeant Jackson replied with a firm shake of his head.

Greer folded his arms, the crinkles in his tan suit outlining the firm slope of his shoulders and neck as he raised his jaw. "Actually, since this is an FBI case, we'll be assuming command over this standoff. Just keep doing what you're doing, but we're going in."

The sergeant turned to face Greer, his own jaw clenching in response. "Look, I've got too much on my hands as it is to get you up to speed. But command has already been given over. The order to keep out—to keep *everyone* out—don't come from me. So if you got a problem with it, take it up with your team lead."

Greer's forehead furrowed in confusion. "Hold on. What team?"

In answer, a throaty voice barked from the far side of the van, "About time you two showed up." Waddling towards them with the focus and fury of an enraged penguin was a wide man in professional pants and office shoes paired with a dark nylon jacket and ballcap, both emblazoned with the bold, stamped letters FBI. Wiping sweat from his brow, Deputy Director Hitchens fixed them with a glare, blinking as though he were unused to the morning sun. "Lucky I got the alert the same time as Merchant. Without someone here to take control, the bastard likely would have slipped your net. Just like the other two!" Here the director waved one of his sausage-like fingers.

"The other two turned themselves in," Sophie replied perplexed at both the deputy director's presence and assertions.

"Exactly!" he shouted back, rolling his eyes as if Sophie were a dim-witted child. "Look, Sergeant Jackson and I have this under control. We don't need you two mucking it up."

"We can't just charge in there," Sophie insisted. "He's a key witness. We think the killer—the *real* killer—is setting these men up. Making them take the fall for him. If we go in guns blazing—"

"They confessed, Quinn!" Director Hitchens roared, spittle flying from his mouth as his face flushed with color. "You think just because you get lucky once, that you're some kind of savant! You're a gimmick, a clown." Hitchens worked his jaw as if he were chewing on something he found particularly bitter and unpleasant. "Merchant told me about your pet theory. What? Are they being hypnotized into confessing? Maybe *you're* the real killer, huh? Is that what you're trying to say. Morons!"

Hitchens spared a fraction of his rant to jam a finger into Greer's lapel as he shouted 'morons', and Sophie watched the former Marine's hands slowly coil and uncoil at his side.

Sophie opened her mouth to respond, but Hitchens cut her off immediately. "They're copycats. Nothing more. Just like any other stupid trend, murders come in waves. Maybe if they see one of these creeps get his head blown off on live TV, we'll make some other bozo think twice."

He's out for blood, Sophie thought in horror, her stomach curdling as her fingernails bit into her palm. He'll kill this young man for no reason stronger than making an example—or just because he knows it's *not* what I want.

At the mention of 'live TV' she saw the news vans. At the edge of the barricades, boom mics were being set up as well-dressed men and women tried to find the best lighting and a position where the morning breeze wouldn't muss their perfectly coifed hair. All around them, people with cellphones were filling the gaps, keeping the police busy with ensuring the line wasn't crossed.

"Give me ten minutes," Sophie asked, trying to keep the desperation from her voice. "It'll take you at least that long to get the SWAT here anyway. Let me try."

"Not happening," Hitchens snapped back.

"Five minutes," Sophie said, her voice rising higher than she intended, her breath coming quicker. "For the love of God, at least give me five minutes before another woman dies!"

"That's enough." Hitchens spun on Quinn. "I don't want to hear another word from you, Quinn. Greer!" Sneering to the tall agent, Hitchens jerked a thumb at Sophie and said, "Would you get a handle on her before I wring her neck?"

And with that, Hitchens stalked away, taking a moment to hike up his pants before turning his wrath on one of the cops nearby.

That was it.

Sophie turned slowly, looking over the hood of the police van to the mechanic's shop. Somewhere inside, Marcus Baker, one of three men who knew the truth, the *only* man who hadn't given a false confession, was counting the seconds until a SWAT team burst in and likely gunned him down.

Their only lead was about to be a red stain on the concrete.

Sophie felt a soft bump behind her shoulder and looked up. Greer had subtly leaned against her. In a low voice, he whispered. "You see that laundromat next door?"

Next to the mechanic shop, sharing a wall on its west side, was a twenty-four-hour laundromat, empty except for a few abandoned baskets and bottles of detergent. Sophie replied in a hushed voice, "Yeah, I see it," casting a glance to make sure Hitchens hadn't decided to come back for round two.

"When I was a Marine engineer, I looked for places like this that could be weak points in defenses. Connected buildings are often cannibalized from older, larger buildings. I'd bet anything there's a forgotten door in the back that runs between them. Maybe locked; at worst, bricked over. We don't have any explosives, so hopefully, it's just a rundown, padlocked door, but... well, we'll figure something out."

Slowly, Sophie saw the connection, what Greer was implying. She put a hand over her pocket, feeling her leather clutch of lockpicks against her chest. Yes, it might work. If she could sneak in from the side.

"What we need is a plan, though," Greer continued. "Now that Hitchens knows we're here—Sophie?"

She was already walking, she gave Greer a final glance and mouthed, 'distract him', then without looking back, Sophie started for the laundromat. She walked with purpose, intentional strides but not hurrying. Nothing that would draw attention.

She heard Greer give a soft curse. Then a few seconds later, she heard Hitchen's toad-like voice in the distance as he hurled a bellowing insult at her partner. She wasn't sure what the ex-Marine engineer had done, but as the laundromat door closed behind her, no one had followed.

Sophie was on her own.

The backroom of the laundromat was locked. The door itself was so flimsy she thought she could simply kick it in, but thankfully the lock was just as cheap, so instead, she inserted a dull bump key, and with a quick knock, forced the handle open.

She had used a couple minutes of the ten she'd tried to beg from Hitchens already, and it took her four more to trace the wall of the laundromat's back room, frustration mounting with every second as her heart sank.

There was no door.

Sophie shoved aside piled boxes and junk accumulated from the maintenance of the washers and dryers out front. But there was nothing. No boarded cupboard or old panel that might conceal a door. Just flat drywall.

That was it then. Like Greer said, they didn't have a demolition charge to blow their way in, not that she would have used it anyway. The point was to save Marcus, not to get shot by scaring him.

With a hopeless sigh, Sophie turned on her heel, leaning back against the wall, letting her head fall back with a dull knock.

A knock?

Sophie's face scrunched in thought, then she turned, giving the wall a few quick taps. She wasn't hearing things. It was hollow.

Without stopping to think, Sophie grabbed a discarded pipe from the pile of junk she'd shifted and began to take heavy, baseball swings at the drywall. It crumbled, falling apart with every stroke, and Sophie soon found herself coughing, holding up her jacket sleeve to cover her nose and mouth as she swung the pipe one-handed.

Wood. Hinges.

It *was* there. Greer's door.

Sophie didn't waste any more time. The hole was big enough for her to squeeze through, and the shoddy padlock was so rusted that it only took one more swing of the pipe to knock it loose. The old wood groaned in protest, and she pulled it back, slowly, carefully.

It was utterly dark beyond, and Sophie pulled up her phone's flashlight to compensate. A rat skittered by as cockroaches fled into the space between the walls. A few old boxes littered the floor along with a broken computer monitor that looked like it was from the eighties.

Sophie crept deeper into what she now assumed to be an old storage room in the back of the mechanic's shop. She'd already crossed the five-minute mark; there was no telling how much time she may have or how quickly Hitchens would press the SWAT team to raid the garage.

Opening the storeroom door, Sophie stepped into a back hallway. She strode cautiously, silently. She didn't really know what sort of mental state Marcus would be in when she found him, but she couldn't imagine it would be pleasant.

She passed a bathroom door, reaching an office with a glass window facing onto the garage floor.

First, she heard a hitching like a hiccup or a stifled sob.

She eased herself around, turning to face the sound. A young man, his head covered in thick, dark curls, looked at her with red eyes, his cheeks glittering in her flashlight's beam from his tears.

The second sound she heard was the click of the revolver's hammer as he leveled the gun at her head.

Chapter15

"Marcus?" Sophie said cautiously.

Turning her palms to show she held nothing but her phone, Sophie stayed where she stood in the dark doorway of the Baker Tire and Repair back office. "I'm Sophie. I'm here to help you."

It had to start with names. Names humanized people, made them feel seen. Saying the dark-haired young man's name might help her reach him. On the flip side, saying her name would make it harder for him to shoot her. She wasn't some nameless, faceless enemy coming for him. She was Sophie now.

Marcus Baker didn't move. He sat against the wall of the office, his knees up in front of him, his arm outstretched to present the cocked revolver while the other held one of his knees like it might try to escape. The streaks of fresh tears on his cheeks and the redness in his eyes showed that he'd been crying, maybe for hours. If he was like the other men, victims of the real killer, he likely would have been drugged overnight. He might have still been confused, definitely scared.

"I saw what happened," Sophie gently explained, "with Eden."

At the mention of his dead girlfriend's name, Marcus flinched, his arm shook and for a moment Sophie thought his trembling hand would pull the trigger whether he meant to or not. Slowly, by inches, Sophie sat down on the floor across from Marcus.

"Marcus, is there anyone else in the garage? Anyone here at all?"

Sophie didn't hear or see any sign of other people. Sergeant Jackson's assertion that Marcus Baker had come here to attack or hold some of his family hostage rang in Sophie's mind, but from everything she could see, there was only one young man sitting alone in the dark.

Her question hung in the air, and Sophie turned her flashlight, leaning it against the wall beside her so that the light shone equally on both of them. It was still extremely dim, but she wanted him to see her face and avoid blinding him.

"Marcus," Sophie tried again. "I know something happened. Something bad. I don't believe it was your fault." Keeping her cadence slow, rhythmic, and loading as much compassion into her words and body language as her skills allowed, Sophie quietly asked, "Will you tell me what happened?"

Silence.

The quiet hitching breath of Marcus' throat, dry from crying.

A lethal clicking creak from the gunmetal as the revolver shook in his hand.

He was completely out of it. Almost catatonic with shock and trauma. Sophie could already see the promise of how this day would haunt Marcus for the rest of his life... however long that might be.

Nearly ten minutes now. If they weren't already here, Hitchens' SWAT team would be showing up soon. She couldn't afford to take all the time Marcus needed; couldn't be as gentle as she should be. His life, and those of other potential victims, might hang in the balance.

Sophie reached into her pocket. Withdrawing the brass pocketwatch, she draped it by its thin chain over the back of her hand, letting the smooth, clean ticking fill the air between them.

"Nothing can hurt you here," Sophie said, opening her throat and speaking from her chest to add weight to the words. "You are safe. Safe from the world. Safe from your own thoughts. They are only smoke. Just pictures." As she spoke, using the rhythm of the ticking watch to set the cadence, she let her own body relax, hoping the example would carry to Marcus.

Slowly, the heavy gun drooped. He blinked, closed his eyes, and with a deep, almost hyperventilating sigh, his shoulders slumped.

"Something happened last night," Sophie prompted. "Tell me about it."

"Romeo," Marcus murmured.

If not for the focused calm she'd woven, Sophie would have jumped. She didn't expect to hear something so near her theory so soon. She took a breath, reminding herself to keep the pace. If she broke the trance too quickly, Marcus could panic. And the gun was still clutched in one hand.

"He called me Romeo," Marcus repeated. "Over and over."

"Who called you Romeo," Sophie asked, softly.

"Don't know. A man in a mask."

A mask? Some killers did use masks, but it was surprisingly uncommon among serial killers. If you go to all the trouble of arranging someone's murder, you don't typically mind if they see you. But then again, he was letting the men go, so that might be reason enough.

"The man in the mask, what does he look like?" Sophie asked. Eleven minutes now. She needed answers fast.

"Just-just a mask. Nothing else. Creepy. The way he talked... like he was, I don't know... British or something, but not really. What he said. It didn't make sense." Marcus' eyes scrunched, his voice rasping as he sucked a quick breath.

"It's ok," Sophie reassured him. "These are just memories." The hypnotic trance was tenuous to begin with, but now, the further he came out of his fugue, the more likely he would snap out of this suggestible state. But there was nothing for it, she needed more. "What did he tell y ou?"

"He told me. 'This is happening. This is happening. Let it happen or it gets worse.'" Marcus blinked rapidly, a fresh tear rolling down his cheek. "I killed her."

Sophie stiffened. Marcus was in a highly suggestible state. If he was lying, it was a lie that was deeply ingrained. Biting her lip anxiously, Sophie knew that she shouldn't say anything that could alter his memory. She had to invite his thoughts. If she asked anything too leading, his mind might latch onto it and mold his memories to make it fit. But it didn't make sense. He had admitted a man in a mask was there.

"I don't think you killed her." Sophie closed her eyes, physically wincing as she said it. She'd either give Marcus the push he needed for a real breakthrough, or she'd just sabotaged everything she was trying to reach.

Marcus went still. Then his chest started heaving. He started hyperventilating, his eyes going wide, he started to look around the room as if some invisible demon were creeping down from the rafters.

"No, no... nonononono," Marcus put his hands to his temples, the revolver now pointed to the ceiling as he rocked back and forth.

"Marcus, listen to me," Sophie scooted closer, risking the movement as she came alongside the young man. "You know what happened. A man in a mask. Tell me what he did."

The young man's fingers knotted in his hair, and he let out a choked sob. "He said, 'you killed her'. He made me repeat it. Made me promise..." Marcus looked up, his gaze meeting Sophie's, she saw he was slipping out of his trance, as she put a hand on his shoulder, his words were now completely voluntary. "He cut Eden's throat. Then he told me I had to tell the cops I'd done it. If I didn't, he said he would kill my baby sister next."

Sophie's mouth hung open. Of course, that was the threat. The killer made them watch him kill, he showed them what he could do, proved it to them. Then he threatened to do it *again* if they didn't confess. He promised to kill Marcus's little sister. Remembering her conversation with Nora Sharpe, how close she was with her brother, how they were the only ones in the family who understood each other. Sophie wondered if the killer had told Sharpe that he'd kill his sister Nora, too. And James Rossi surely had someone in his life that he'd go to prison to protect.

They failed to protect the women they loved, and they just didn't want to lose anyone else.

So they lied.

"You have to save her," Marcus said, his hand coming up to Sophie's shoulder, matching her grip. "Promise me. Promise me he won't get my little sister."

"I promise," Sophie said. And with a spike of fear in her heart, she hoped it was a promise she could keep. "Come on." Pulling Marcus's shoulder, Sophie stood. "There are cops outside, but if you give me that gun, we'll get you—"

Sophie's words were cut off by the sound of shattering glass.

A flash of white light flared as a sound like a shotgun exploded in her ear.

A flash-bang grenade. The SWAT team was here.

Disoriented. Blind. Deaf. Sophie moved on instinct.

She grabbed Marcus, dragging him behind her as she threw her palms to the sky.

Chapter 16

A burst of pain shot through Sophie's skull. She let out a small cry as an icy sensation stiffened her spine.

"Oof, sorry." Greer half whispered his apology as he settled the cold pack he'd applied to Sophie's head.

"Thanks, I got it." With a groan, Sophie took over, shifting the frozen bag of coolant gel over the stiff bruise on the top of her head. Getting flash-banged and clothes-lined to the concrete floor by a SWAT team wasn't the most unpleasant she'd ever felt, but at the moment, it was a strong contender.

The noise in the FBI field office made her ears ache, but Greer had managed to find an unoccupied conference room where they could dim the lights and talk without having to shout, though, the air conditioner periodically whirred up with aggravating enthusiasm from its roost in the exterior wall. With the window blinds closed, the long table and metal framed chairs were striped with golden orange bars of afternoon sun.

Setting aside his cell phone, Greer said, "I just got word. Local PD has uniforms watching Marcus's family. His sister accepted protective custody, so she's being watched at the station. Safe as she can be under the circumstances."

"Good." Sophie let out a sigh of relief. "I was worried they might refuse. How's Marcus holding up?"

Sitting back, Greer bobbed his head noncommittally. "He waited until the lawyer arrived, but then his story matched what you told us all. Hitchens is still raising Caine over how it all went down, but he can't exactly complain that everyone *survived.*"

At least not where people can hear, Sophie thought, though the words were swallowed in another throb of pain from her head. She still had some pain killers from the last time she'd been hospitalized and knew they would be kicking in soon, but the waiting was still... uncomfortable.

Greer frowned, a look of concern furrowing his forehead.

"I'm fine," Sophie murmured. "The killer's not going to slow down just because I cracked my head."

Her partner still looked unconvinced, but Sophie cut in before he could vocalize his protests. "Ok, so what do we know? One, the killer wears a mask. From Marcus' description, it sounds like a weeping human face of some kind."

Opening the case file, Greer nodded along. "He also talks with some kind of strange cadence or accent."

"Marcus said it possibly sounded 'British', but that could mean a lot of things," Sophie interjected.

Greer rolled his fingers across the tabletop, thinking for a moment. "He's leaving Classics: Shakespeare, the *Iliad*. Maybe he's trying to affect that way of speaking?"

"It's possible," Sophie admitted. "We can follow up with Marcus and see if he recalls any specific phrasing, but from the little he told me while I had him in a trance, it sounded like modern English." She chewed her lip, shifting the cool pack as a rivulet of melting frost snaked an icy finger down the back of her neck. "The books are the key, though. I'm sure of it."

"And couples," Greer said distantly. "Always couples."

Sophie sat forward; as she did, her head pulsed with a fresh wave of pain, and she slipped. There was a moment of vertigo, and she had dropped the ice pack to grab the table beside her when she felt Greer's hands catch her by the shoulders. With a sure strength, he helped her sit back in her chair, gently, but firmly guiding her away from her attempt to pick up the cool pack; only bending down to fetch it himself when he was sure she was securely in her seat.

"You're sure you don't have a concussion?"

Sophie smirked. "No. But we have a killer to catch, so I'm not sure how it's relevant."

For a moment, the blue-eyed FBI agent's mouth drew into a hard line, then he closed his eyes and folded his hands over his mouth, dragging his fingertips across his stubbled cheeks as he said. "You know, Miss Quinn, I hope I'm not overstepping when I say I would sincerely prefer that you *not* die in the line of duty."

With a wink, Sophie coyly replied, "I'll do my best, but no promises."

Greer looked away, turning to face the blinds as the moment stretched into awkward silence.

Sophie's grin faded. "The EMTs said I should be ok, but to go to the hospital if I get nauseous or start having trouble focusing."

"It's not just about that," Greer replied, a faint rebuke in his voice. "It's these unilateral decisions. Running off on your own. Risking our lives is part of the job, but—no, actually, it's part of *my* job. You're a consultant, not even an agent."

Sophie winced at the phrase. After Molly's death, she'd thrown away everything, pursued a double PhD in an obsessive time-frame, turned her whole life to the study of men like the River Killer in the hopes of joining the FBI, of getting to be on the team that would take him down. Due to her flashbacks... her *instability*, they turned her down, leaving her to beg, borrow, and steal the access she could get as a consultant.

From the expression on Greer's face, he had also realized how his words could be taken. A quick turn of the head, a shift in the eyes and hands. Sophie saw the tell-tale body language of an apology that failed to be spoken. Instead, the agent said, "We're supposed to be a team. And I find that, more often, I'm just running to catch up with whatever decision you've already made. I want to help you. But you have to work with me—and not just when it's convenient for you."

Sophie's face was getting hot. She blinked as her gut clenched. When it was convenient for her?

"I made a call," Sophie said. She felt her voice was tight, but she didn't care. "You heard Hitchens. We had to act fast or our witness was going to end up dead. The only reason we have any hope of a lead is because I acted."

Greer sat up, he locked eyes with Sophie, his own expression as implacable as hers. "I'm not questioning the decision. It probably *was* the best option. But what if it hadn't been?" Greer lifted a hand, giving quick, emphasizing chops to the air in front of his chest as he said, "You are courageous and smart and capable, but you run around as if you're bullet-proof, and you're not. If you get hurt—or killed—you're not the only one it affects."

"Well, maybe I should be."

The words stuck in the air like a dart pinning them both to their seats. To be truthful, Sophie wasn't entirely sure what she'd meant. She'd snapped out the words without really thinking. But as they lingered, she realized it was the truth. Her life didn't belong to anyone else and if she wanted to gamble it, it was her business and no one else's.

The air conditioner whirred to life, and a burst of cool air washed over the pair, kicking up a loose strand of Sophie's hair and sticking it to the wet cold pack.

"Maybe I'm better on my own," Sophie murmured. "I can't stop killers if I'm scared of who's going to be sad or upset or hurt if I get killed."

Greer looked to the door, rubbing his palms together slowly, working out a kink in one of his knuckles. For a moment Sophie thought he might simply leave. Instead, he quietly said, "Have you thought that maybe keeping people at arm's length is what hurts them more?" Swallowing, the tall agent rolled his neck, still looking anywhere but at Sophie. "If you keep everyone away so they don't get hurt when you die... what's the difference between that and already being dead?"

Sophie's mouth hung open. She could feel her face flushing, and her jaw absently worked as her mind reached for an answer. She didn't care about being right anymore, and a bitter part of her was reaching for some cutting reply, something that would hurt her partner, that would make him see he just needed to get away from her.

But she couldn't... because she didn't actually want him to go.

For better or worse, before Sophie could settle on a reply, Greer stood. He vaguely gestured to the hall. "I'm going to take a walk. Clear my head. I'll swing by the cafeteria on the way back, so if you want anything feel free to shoot me a text."

Nodding absently, Sophie sat in silence until the door closed.

She wanted to be mad. She wanted to label the older agent a smug, self-righteous prick. But she knew it wasn't true. He just didn't want her to die. She thought about her mother and father, the way they buried their heads in the sand after Molly's death. It was the same with them... they just don't want to lose their other daughter, too. Sophie leaned forward, resting her forehead on the now mildly-chill cold pack with her elbows on her knees.

The determined bleed for what they want; the obsessed make everyone else bleed.

Sophie had latched onto the phrase to explain the half-mad focus of her investigation into the River Killer. She didn't use people; all the sacrifices she made were her own to make. She'd given up her wealth, her status, her cushy life in California. She'd burned everything she had in the hope that it would bring RK into her sights—even her relationship with her parents.

The obsessed don't care who they hurt. That wasn't her. But if she took it too far... if she did get killed... An image rose in Sophie's mind of her mother's worried look, bending over her father in the hospital bed. Only it wasn't her father, no, her daddy was beside Mama, now, comforting her, and instead of a hospital bed, it was a casket.

Gritting her teeth, Sophie tried to banish her doubt. It was like Gavriel had told her. Right or wrong, she *knew* what direction her compass pointed, and she couldn't do anything but follow it.

But maybe she didn't need to follow it alone? Maybe there was a compromise.

Sophie took out her phone. Cycling down her contact list, she found her mother's number. The afternoon light set a glare over the screen, making Sophie blink and squint. All she had to do was push 'call'. She could start making things right, right now.

...

No. With a groan, Sophie slammed her phone on the table. Her heart twisted inside her chest, and she thought of the men she'd seen these last two days. The pain in their eyes. No. All this would do for her is invite tragedy.

Tragedy.

Sophie's eyes flew wide. Of course, that was the connection.

"He wants to make Tragedies." Sophie reached for her laptop bag and pulled up the case files. The killer's mask, a weeping mask—it was one of the two classic Grecian masks: Comedy and Tragedy, the kind still used as decorations in old theaters. He was leaving classic books, classic tragedies with doomed romances.

"The books are the key," Sophie repeated to herself. reviewing the evidence files.

They were not off-the-shelf new, and she was right that they were not left over from some high school English class. They fit in at the wealthy home of Josephine Ramsey and Jonathan Sharpe and stuck out like a broken leg at Marcus Baker's apartment.

A collector, a specialist book store. Someone with a history of violence, perhaps?

Piece by bloody piece, a profile of the killer began to coalesce in Sophie's mind, and she sorted the FBI databases she had access too, filtering, refining. Losing herself in the search, she only got up once, to adjust the blinds as the afternoon sun began to cut a harsh glare into her eyes.

Sophie didn't notice Greer's return until he set a crinkling bag next to her.

"I didn't hear from you, but I got you the chicken parm, and—what's this?" He leaned down, focusing over her shoulder at the laptop screen.

"Hunter Barnes," Sophie said, then sending an address to her phone, she slapped the computer closed and stood, leaving the flaccid ice pack behind.

No headrush. No dizziness. Only a mild throbbing now. She was ready.

"Who is that?" Greer asked.

But Sophie was already headed to the door. "No time. I'll explain on the way... On second thought." Turning on her heel, Sophie snatched up the bag with the melty, chicken sandwich Greer had brought her. "We'll eat in the car. And don't worry—" Giving her partner a wide-mouthed smile, Sophie held up her pinkie, "I won't leave you behind this time. Promise."

Chapter 17

In a room full of old books and loose papers, candles are an exceedingly bad idea. But the Mask found he couldn't help himself. The aesthetic was worth the risk of a fiery death.

"So many choices..." he murmured. The photo paper rasped as he dragged it across his desk by his fingertips, rearranging it between two other photographs.

The room had an off-kilter feel to it, as if it were gently spinning around him. It was the shadows, the flickering, dancing ghosts thrown over the stuffed furniture and floor-to-ceiling bookshelves that surrounded his desk in the windowless room. Three candles were insufficient to fully cast out the gloom, but it was enough for him to read by.

"Lancelot and Guinevere. Your affair destroyed a kingdom, broke the trust and spirit of the legendary Arthur of Camelot..." He rolled his fingers over a shot of a woman in dark sunglasses as she sat with a man who was not her husband at a café out of town. "The betrayal is delicious. Love and lust fighting for her soul as Lancelot's will withers under the flame of his desire for her. Isn't that a much better story? A more elevated story?"

Taking a silver marker, the Mask drew a simple sword at the man's hip, then he traced a silver crown around the woman's head, gesturing over his shoulder as if calling for a response from an invisible audience. "Left alone, their story would be dreadful. He, slaking his lust until he's bored with her. She, merely playing at escape before returning to the stability of her husband. Even if she did leave him for her new flame, within a year he would no longer be Lancelot to her. They will never be as passionate or powerful as they are now."

Glancing to the next photo, he stood, pacing the room with his hands clasped behind his back. His voice rose in stern declarations, "And what of Aeneas and Dido?" The Mask admired his own work, surprising himself with his photographic artistry as he captured the very moment the beautiful Dido had her heart broken, her strong Aeneas leaving her... it was almost profane to call such a moment a mere 'break up'. It was sacred, as heartbreaking as a ship lost at sea. But left alone, she would recover. She would drown her sorrows in ice cream and late-night phone calls or throw herself into her work.

"It would be a waste!" he railed, the candles guttering around him as he flailed an arm dramatically. "She is on the point of true transcendence—to elevate her experience. But she will never throw herself on a pyre like Dido. Someone must help her along." The Mask ran his fingers through his hair, smoothing it back, and taking a heady breath of the warm air.

"And you... fair-voiced Orpheus—"

A digital chirp interrupted him, and the Mask's lips twisted in a snarl. "Poor stage-craft to interrupt a man mid-monologue," he muttered opening his cell phone.

He had set alerts on various search sites and apps. If he was to make good on his promises, he would need to know if his tragic heroes broke their word. Marcus Baker, Romeo. His name appeared in highlighted yellow on the screen. The young man had certainly put up a greater fight than the previous two. One of the advantages of youth, the Mask supposed. If anyone was going to resist his threat, it may be his young Romeo. Impetuous and rash.

Marcus Baker, 20, was arrested this morning after a standoff with police outside a Baton Rouge mechanic's shop. The young man is the prime suspect in the murder of Eden Garza, 19, his girlfriend, who was found dead this morning in Baker's apartment. Police have declined to offer comment on Baker's motives, but inside sources say Garza's murder may be connected to other recent murders. The FBI were on scene for Baker's arrest—

The Mask scrolled over a picture of a corpulent, sweating man in a blue FBI jacket and ballcap. Had someone given up the secret? He stared through the screen, his eyes distant as he speculated on what this could mean.

Flicking through the report, his eyes rapidly drank the information as quickly as it passed. No specific mention of Cleopatra or Helen. They may be getting suspicious, but they are still far off. If they arrested Baker, then they must not know the truth yet.

But they may soon.

Stepping back to his photographs, the Mask pocketed his phone and ran his fingers over the old volumes arrayed on his desk, lifting them, smelling the old ink on dry paper. Guinevere. Eurydice. Dido.

Yes, the police may not see his hand in things yet. But they will. If the FBI is involved, they will.

So I must get as much done as I can, he mused. Before my own story comes to its own tragic conclusion.

Chapter 18

"He could be dangerous. We should wait until the shop clears out a bit more," Sophie said conspiratorially.

Parked across the street from Garden Books, the setting sun was beginning to sink below the buildings at their back. Foot traffic was light but consistent, crossing from the parking garage to the restaurants and boutiques further up the road. Only a few people came and went from the hole-in-the-wall bookseller, but behind the front windows, Sophie could see at least a half-dozen still perusing the stacks.

Greer had the file Sophie found open on his phone, reading aloud as he stole glances at the shop and adjacent alleyways. "Public lewdness, indecent exposure, disorderly conduct... Run it by me again," Greer asked, winding his finger in the air. "The guy is a creep for sure, but you think he's drugging and murdering these women?"

"Look at the out-of-state records." Sophie frowned. Nearly eight o'clock and the sun was almost set; the shop would be closing soon. Why were so many people still milling around? Turning back to Greer she elaborated. "Hunter Barnes was part of the Mississippi Shakespeare Troupe."

"So he has some history with the classics?" Greer said, scrolling further into the file.

"Tons," Sophie confirmed. "Until he was kicked out six years ago."

Greer whistled, his eyebrows going wide for a moment as he found the next section of the file. "He attacked one of his castmates with a knife, a young woman. Looks like there were also sexual assault allegations but no charges."

"No. He only did time for the attack with the knife. After he got out, we have a change of address to Baton Rouge, and shortly after that, he started working here."

Greer bent low, his tall frame craning to see out of Sophie's window as he looked into Garden Books. "Let me guess, they have a section for older editions and collectibles."

"Just like the kind we've been finding at the crime scenes."

Greer's expression settled into hard focus, the velvet rasp of his voice rumbling as he said, "You're right. We should wait until the shop clears out a bit more."

* * *

No matter how many she did, stakeouts always unsettled Sophie.

Her nerves had been honed on the focused precision of stage shows. Sharp timeframes and cues. Curtain up at 7:15 on the dot. Close countdowns where she knew when to start her preparation and exactly when she could relax.

But here, in the real world, things didn't happen that way. She might be sitting for a few minutes or several days. The hour she chose to break off and get food or the second it took her to look away and stretch her neck could be the moment something happened, the moment she needed to be there. It frayed at her anxiety in a way she'd never fully conquered. And as the minutes ticked by, Sophie drew out the deck of cards from her pocket if only to have something to fidget with.

Simply missing that single card she'd given to the mob boss, the deck felt off. Uneven. Still, she shuffled it, keeping her hands busy rolling the cards back and forth, turning them in intricate patterns and designs before collapsing them back with a buzzing riffle. Letting her nervous energy pour into the motion of her fingers to keep her eyes on the bookstore.

Her back was getting stiff from the awkward angle and she groaned as she rolled her shoulders.

"You know, I'm watching too. You can look away for a second. No need to break your neck."

Sophie glanced to her partner, and Greer shot her a quick wink, taking up her vigil as she rubbed the tendons in her neck.

Their previous conversation came to mind, back in the field office, and Sophie felt a flush of embarrassment. "Thanks," she said quietly.

Despite his criticism and complaints, Greer was still here. He'd listened to her when she gave him the suspect's address. He had picked up what was bothering her and stepped up so she didn't get a crick in her neck. It was a small thing, but it was one more little thing that was adding up to a big statement about the good-looking, older man. He walked his talk. In his eyes, they were a team still.

"I'm sorry," Sophie said. She turned her shoulder, leaning against her door just a little bit to catch Greer's eye as he stared into the suspect's bookshop. He was hesitant, his shoulders tightening just a little. "I was thinking about what you said," Sophie continued, "And about how I've been doing things over the last six years. I don't know if Merchant told you, but the reason I've been in Detroit the last couple years is because I took things too far. I got another agent hurt."

She swallowed, admitting the full truth, thinking about it for the first time in a long time was painful. "There were other reasons," Sophie continued. "I stole files. Lied to people about what I was doing. But that was the trigger. He had to retire because of me. I was obsessed with catching RK. I needed to catch him... and I still do. But I had to get my head right." She picked at the edges of her cards with her fingernails, letting them snap together softly. "The determined bleed for what they want; the obsessed make everyone else bleed. I say that a lot, in my head," Sophie felt her cheeks flush at the embarrassing admission but pushed on, "I don't want other people to get hurt for what I have to do. I don't want to use people... but I can't let RK go either. I can't let any of them go. They have to pay for what they've done. They have to pay for what they did to my family. To my sister. To *me.*"

Sophie turned back to the shop, using the excuse to hide the stiff anger in her expression. But in the glass of her door's window, she caught her own reflection as well as the solemn, sympathetic look etched in Greer's hard features.

"Losing someone, being around death, it changes you," the big man rumbled, the words sounding heavy, dragged up from his chest by e-ffort. "I never had a sister," he said. "But I lost men I called brother. I understand what it's like to be caught in a fight you didn't choose. To know that if you don't do everything you can, that evil is just going to go on hurting people, giving others the same sort of pain you're going through. How it keeps you up at night."

Greer lay his palm over Sophie's shoulder, his calloused hand as light as a bird as he gave her a reassuring squeeze. "I meant what I said before, Miss Quinn. You're one of the strongest people I've ever met. You're... amazing." There was pain in his voice, held in check, but definitely there. But also hope. "Your battle is my battle," Greer said gently. "I trust you, and I just want you to trust me too."

Without thinking, Sophie leaned into the former Marine's touch, her head tilting as if to lay her cheek over his hand like a pillow but stopping short. Shifting in her seat, Sophie turned to look into Greer's clear, blue eyes, past the care and the worry, into the compassion he was offering.

"I trust you," she said.

A crooked smile cracked on his face, and Sophie returned the expression.

The phone in her pocket buzzed, and the pair both took sharp breaths as if suddenly waking from a dream.

Greer looked past her to the bookstore, "Looks like a couple more are filing out. Two more at the register. We should be able to move in a couple more minutes.

Sophie stowed her cards and opened her phone nodding in understanding. "Probably Merchant looking for an—" She stopped mid-thought.

It was a simple message forwarded from the encrypted app on her laptop. The insider, the man from the Mississippi Line Minutemen, and her best link to the River Killer.

Rou Morte Bayou. 1 hr.

No money, no info.

A set of coordinates followed. Sophie recognized the place; her obsessive knowledge of the riverways around New Orleans and the Louisiana delta quickly calculated how quickly she could get there.

One hour. It was possible, just.

But she'd have to convince Greer to give her the car—

She'd have to leave the investigation.

"What is it?" Greer asked, his concern obvious behind the words, but the man himself was too much of a gentleman to try and read her screen.

For a moment, it felt as though her heart had stopped. If she didn't take this chance, would she ever have another? These cloak-and-dagger exchanges were extremely risky on both sides. If she declined, would he take a chance to try to meet her again? But if she left, the killer may strike again tonight… she would be abandoning Greer.

I trust you. Her own words echoed in her head as her stomach tightened in a nauseous, thorny knot. Why now? It was too cruel. But there was no changing what it was.

"…nothing," Sophie said delicately, her face a mask of indifference and mild annoyance as her mind screamed for her to stop. Instead, she typed: *I need more time.* And closed her phone.

Chapter 19

"Where did he go?"

Sophie squinted into the bookstore's front window, the streetlights joining the waning orange-pink of the setting sun to help illuminate the interior now that half the shopfloor lights had been turned out. "There are still two customers there, he can't have left."

Their suspect, bookshop owner Hunter Barnes, had stepped away from the register five minutes before and had not yet returned. A younger man, wiry with mousey brown hair in a modest button-up and overlarge glasses, had turned the shop sign from open to closed and flipped a switch near the door to dim the lights.

"They can't close up with two customers in there," Sophie repeated curiously.

"One customer," Greer said grimly. "The other one stepped by that large stack and hasn't come back yet either."

"You don't think...?"

"No." Greer worked his jaw, his sky blues narrowed in thought. "It's not his MO to take people. The murders are in the victims' own homes."

He was right, but that still left Sophie with the puzzle of what was happening in Garden Books. "Now the other one has gone over to that stack," she pointed out.

The second customer, a blonde woman perhaps a little older than Sophie, ambled over to the row of books the first customer had disappeared behind, and then she was gone too.

The younger man stepped to the register and started in on what appeared to Sophie to be simple bookkeeping for the shop. But in that same moment, a man in a trench coat appeared at the shop door, simply letting himself in as though the closed sign were not there.

"What on earth?" Greer murmured.

"I know," Sophie agreed. "A Louisiana summer is also a bit hot for a trench coat, don't you think?"

The trench coat waved to the young man, who waved back, both of them short, subtle waves from the hip, and then the coated man made his way to the back of the shop as well.

Within the space of five minutes, three more appeared. A man and two women, each in unseasonal coats or wide-brimmed hats that seemed like caricatures of spies from the 1950s rather than actual disguises. Each gave a similar wave to the man at the register, and each received the same gesture in return.

"Their fingers," Sophie said abruptly. She hadn't seen it at first, but starting with the second man, she saw that their fingers were not flat or spread in a simple wave, but oddly clutched, crooked, and hooked into a sort of sign. "They're giving some sort of secret symbol, like a password."

"A cult?" Greer's mouth hung open, dumbfounded. "It's not unheard of, but serial killers are usually loners. It's rare for them to work together, to... organize." He turned up a palm and waved at the shop in disbelief. But Sophie was nodding along with him.

"The killer is in a mask, and we still don't know enough. It might be part of some initiation or a role passed between people."

"Christ," Greer said through clenched teeth. "We can't let them scatter. I'm calling for backup."

Sophie nodded. "Good idea. But we're running out of time too." Glancing at the deep purple running down over the last dregs of sunset, Sophie said, "The killings happen in the evenings, appropriate for a late dinner. The person in the mask may already be out getting ready for his next killing. If the people inside know anything, we need to find out as quickly as possible."

Greer clenched a fist, rolling his knuckles. She could tell he didn't like the idea, but after only a moment he gave a resigned sigh. "Ok. You keep an eye on the front and organize our backup when they get here. I'll go around back and make sure no one escapes through an alleyway door."

"I can't just watch." Sophie insisted, an edge in her voice. Licking her lips thoughtfully, she pointed to the man at the register. "They're using a gesture. That means they don't recognize each other by sight. I can bluff my way in, find out what they're doing. I can find out if the killer is out there tonight. Maybe even find out who he's after."

"It's too dangerous," Greer replied. "If they find out you're with the FBI, you'll be surrounded. They won't hesitate to take you down." Glancing down at his phone, Greer quickly interjected. "Backup will be here in twenty minutes."

"It could be too late by then," Sophie locked eyes with her partner, staring up at the big man as she set her jaw. "Blending in is what I do. And I have my pistol if anything goes wrong. This is the right call. Trust me."

Greer met her stare, the air between them feeling alive and electric as neither gave any sign of backing down. Then, with an explosive sigh, Greer opened his door. "Fine. But if I hear anything, I'm kicking down the door to get you, backup or not."

"Deal," Sophie said, sliding out of her seat.

The pair split off immediately, and in a couple dozen hustled steps, Greer disappeared into the alleyway beside the shop.

The mousey-haired young man smoothed his Christmas-green vest over his button-up as the bell over the shop door tinkled. When he saw Sophie approach, his eyes lit up for a moment in what looked like delighted surprise. And for a reason Sophie couldn't pinpoint, the stare filled her with a feeling as though a hundred invisible insects were crawling over her.

Suppressing her shudder, Sophie stopped, her eyes lingering on the back of the shop. "Is Hunter here?" she lifted her hand to her waist, her fingers crooking to match the gesture she'd seen. Her digits were dexterous enough to mimic anything the other visitors did, so Sophie simply hoped she'd seen it clearly enough to be an accurate forgery.

The bookshop clerk gave her an enthusiastic smile. "First time, huh?"

Sophie considered the odd non-sequitur, then returned the young man's smile with her own, deciding to add a trace of nervous energy by bouncing her knees and shrugging. "Is it that obvious?" she joked, looking for any sign of deception or malice in the clerk's body language.

"No, it's just that newcomers like to know there is a familiar face there. I won't ask how you and the boss met," he said with a wink. "Just know that it's ok to be nervous. Everyone in there had a first time too. But once you're in the circle, once you experience it..." giving a waggle of his eyebrows, the young man leaned forward in a conspiratorial whisper, "It's like nothing else."

There was something unsavory in the young man's tone, and Sophie felt her stomach drop. Perhaps they weren't too far from their theory. Maybe the masked killer wasn't one person, it was a shared experience, a dozen or more people, a growing circle thirsty for murder. Could this young man have been the hand that cut Maya Rossi's throat? Josephine Ramsey's? or Eden Garza's? There was nothing 'British' about his inflection. Just the native drag and skip of someone raised near the mouth of the mighty Mississippi. But that didn't mean he couldn't have been behind another killing.

Not sure what else to say to the young man, Sophie gave him a final anxious grin, using the natural anxiety bruiting through her veins to play the role of nervous neonate. Turning, she walked to the back of the shop.

"Just remember to pace yourself," the young man called after her. "It can get messy back there."

Sophie discretely checked her gun, comforted by the metallic weight under her coat.

Behind the row of books was a unisex bathroom and a plain brown door, painted to blend with the wall and labeled with a brass plaque that read 'Employees Only'. Taking a gamble, Sophie pushed open the employee entry.

Darkness.

As her eyes adjusted, Sophie made out the shapes of candles. Three tea-lights flickering on the floor, one sitting at the foot of yet another door. Following the little light, she saw more warm firelight seeping beneath the threshold, and the gentle sound of classical music from the other side. She remembered the crime scenes, the melted candles left to burn all night, the repeating music turned off and cataloged by the forensics techs.

Was this where it all started?

A hand clapped onto her shoulder from the darkness behind her.

"Where do you think you're going?"

Chapter 20

One hand going for the gun in her coat, Sophie whirled around.

"Whoa! Whoa! Easy."

Her hand froze, still hidden under her suit jacket, and the man in front of her had put his hands up in a placating gesture.

He wore shadowy robes, black or some deep blue-violet that seemed to bleed into the darkness around him. Over his face was a white mask. It may have been porcelain, but by the flimsy look of the strap, Sophie guessed it may be plastic painted with a glossy glaze. His features were completely hidden behind that mask, and as the shadows fell over it, Sophie saw that it was ridged with deep, finger-thick curls that seemed to pull the eyes and frozen lips in odd directions.

It would be easy enough to read weeping into the mask's features... or laughing or sneering... the ambiguity gave it an almost insane quality that left Sophie guessing at the mask-maker's intentions.

Tilting his head, the masked man said, "There's steps to follow, remember." Gesturing into the darkness behind him, Sophie saw a dark curtain she'd missed before. Behind it, one of the tea light candles showed a table with folded robes and a wall set with masks on hooks.

Greer's words returned to Sophie's mind. You put on a mask, and it lets you do things you'd never do.

A heavy hand fell on Sophie's shoulder, giving her a firm, almost massaging press as the man ushered her towards the curtain. After her first step, he let go and disappeared behind the door she'd attempted to enter a moment ago, slipping in so quickly, she only caught the barest glimmer of the rich candlelight beyond.

Ok, Sophie thought, stepping to the table. So robes and masks are mandatory? If people came in one at a time and put on disguises in this nearly perfect dark, she could understand why there was at least *some* level of anonymity in the group.

The masks themselves were in an obscene variety. Goat horns and laughing cherubs, pointed-chinned devils and almost featureless faces. Some were closer to Mardi Gras masks and encrusted with costume jewelry like Venetian carnival masks.

And hanging off to one side, hung a pair of familiar masks, the Grecian pair: Laughing Comedy and Weeping Tragedy. Her heart raced, and Sophie shot a nervous glance to the door. What was going on here?

For a moment, Sophie considered taking the weeping mask. It could be evidence, but she would need something she could wear and if there was DNA, her own skin and breath could contaminate it. Instead, she took the nearly-flat 'blank' mask, missing even a slit for the mouth.

Grabbing a loose-fitting robe, she wrapped it over her clothing, cinching it off with the connected belt and pulling it tight around her throat. The sleeves were loose and billowy, so she took a moment to free her gun, hiding it in one hand beneath her robe.

There. That was it. That was all she could think to do. Sophie closed her eyes, taking a deep breath to level out her heart, to stop her thoughts from running riot. She imagined Greer outside the bookstore, checking the alleyway and backstreet for exists. If her mental picture was correct, the room beyond this door would share a wall with the back of the building, but she'd have to go in to be sure. Would he be able to hear her if she shouted for him? She reassured herself it wouldn't come to that.

Stepping to the door, Sophie tightened her grip on her concealed pistol.

No, it won't come to that. No matter what happens beyond this door, I will blend in. I will get my answers.

Gripping the doorknob, Sophie pushed her way in.

A dozen or so robed and masked figures clustered around a room covered from one end to the other in ornate carpets. They covered the walls and floor, layered on each other at strange almost careless angles. One side of the room seemed to fade and curl into shadow with an eclectic smattering of couches, stuffed chairs, and ottomans. On the room's opposite side, a long table dominated the wall.

Incense burned in stone holders on the table, filling the air with a strange mix of sage and patchouli. Around it lay open bowls of what looked at first like candy, but as Sophie stepped further into the room, she saw that they were actually pills. Oblong and round, engraved and printed.

Her eidetic memory started trying to catalog them, but she pulled her attention away. She didn't need to know exactly what they were to see from the first few that it was a mix of sedatives, amphetamines, and pain killers. She thought of the drugged wine at Josephine Ramsey's crime scene.

The next bowl arrested her focus again, and Sophie's eyes went wide behind her mask to see a deep salad bowl of sliced, dried mushrooms. And unless the dim light was deceiving her, they were the psychedelic variety. Beside the bowls, seeming tame by comparison, was a large water pipe, smoldering from some recent use. Glass bottles and grinders of potent-smelling cannabis rested beside it.

Some of the masked figures held wine glasses, and three large bottles, one already opened, stood on the same table as the incense and drugs. The atmosphere was a dinner party diluted with the essence of a hookah lounge and a Halloween masquerade.

For a terrifying moment, Sophie thought the room had only a single entrance and exit, a bottle with only one narrow way out. But as she looked to the far wall, the tightness in her chest relaxed. An old double door, barely obscured by a translucent drape, was set in the wall she knew faced the backstreet behind the shop. She didn't see any obvious locks on it. Good. At bare minimum, it was one more chance for her to escape and a likely place to find Greer if she needed him. Assuming he'd found his way to this back door and not some other side entrance.

In their robes, Sophie had difficulty parsing the assembled cultists from one another. She knew that Hunter Barnes was a heavyset man if not overly tall, and she tried to pick him out. It occurred to Sophie as she did, that the man in the ambiguous mask, who had stopped her outside the door, may have *been* Hunter Barnes without her realizing, and the thought unnerved her.

She nodded subtly to the people around her. And they inclined their heads in return. Oddly, it felt as if they were all playing the same game. Pretending to belong without really knowing each other. Sophie stepped to the table, and took a pill, palming it as she pretended to swallow. If she was going to blend in, she may as well do it properly.

The door to the room opened once more, and this time, Sophie immediately identified the man who stepped inside. Despite also donning a robe and disguise, the young clerk from the entrance had put his overlarge glasses on *over* his mask.

The room fell quiet.

The large man from the hall asked in a voice heavy, with the cadence of ritual, "Do the wolves howl tonight?"

Raising his palms, the young man lifted his voice in answer, "The door is barred. The night is come. None intrude upon our revels."

"And are all assembled of one mind?" the thickly ridged mask called out to the room.

"We are," said the group, with Sophie doing her best to let her voice quietly join the chorus. She was not alone as some seemed as surprised as her and followed the young clerk's lead with a small echo of delay. Among them, his voice rang out the clearest.

"Good," the ridged mask said, stepping to the center of the room. His voice was more casual, more conversational. "We are here to experience life. To take and drink deeply of all the experiences it can give us. We are the truly free, the elevated and enlightened. Here to step beyond the limits imposed by this prison we call society." The longer he spoke, the more convinced Sophie was that this was the man she was looking for, the leader of this little circle and owner of the bookshop, Hunter Barnes. As he spat the word 'limits' and 'society', he lifted the bottom of his mask, barely revealing his lips as he reached to the bowl of mushrooms and took a sliver, sucking it enthusiastically before he swallowed.

"No shame. No fear," Barnes continued, uncorking a bottle of wine. "We are masters of our universe."

Around the room were murmured words of approval. An anticipatory energy, like the hum in the air before a lightning strike. All around her, the robed cultists were whispering, looking between each other.

Were they about to select a new killer? To announce their next target? Sophie adjusted her grip on her pistol.

"So... Let us begin!"

At those words, there was a flurry of movement, and for a panicked second, Sophie didn't know where to look, a spike of fear set her heart going again.

Then came the confusion.

All around her, robes were falling to the ground, tossed to the carpeted floor or onto the furniture. Unlike her, however, not one of the assembly had kept a stitch of their own clothing on beneath.

In the space of a few giggling laughs and whoops, Sophie Quinn was the only clothed person in a room full of naked, masked men and women.

"I've made a terrible mistake," Sophie murmured to herself, power-walking back to the room's entrance.

It wasn't a secret murder cult. It was a *sex* cult. An orgy club. A psychedelic, hedonistic swingers group, and she'd been so focused on finding a killer, she'd missed all the signs.

"Hey, are you ok?"

A figure stepped in front of Sophie. Clad in only a mask under his oversized glasses, yet for some reason still wearing his socks, it was the clerk.

"I'm sorry, I shouldn't be here," Sophie said hurriedly, trying to step around the younger man, but he held up a hand, stepping with her like a choreographed dance step.

"I get it. You're new, you're nervous. But think how brave it was for you to come here to begin with? Just give it a few minutes, have a drink." The clerk's voice was gentle and encouraging, and it may have been endearing if not for the sights and sounds of eleven other people already pairing off into two and threes around her.

"That's not what I mean," Sophie said. "There's been a mistake."

Sophie was by no means squeamish about the human body. She's shared plenty of dressing rooms over the years, and she was used to the decided lack of privacy in showbusiness. She'd been a magician's assistant, tights and corsets included, and in the early years of her solo career, a revealing costume was just one of many tools she'd used to get people's attention. Even when she was successful, she'd been to more than one party where things had gotten... out of hand. In many ways, Hollywood deserved its reputation, in her opinion.

But the pure focus and intent of these people was wild to see.

The room behind her was getting rowdy, and she heard a woman let out a shrill scream of delight.

"Step aside," she said to the young clerk.

"You can leave if you want. But if you don't take the plunge, I think you'll regret it," he replied, stroking Sophie's shoulder.

"Move," she snapped, venom in her voice.

"Alright, alright, geez—" As the young man's hand came away, Sophie heard a loud *BOOM* from the far side of the room. All heads turned to look, as a second calamitous, *BOOM* sounded, accompanied by a *crack!*

"Oh, no," Sophie whispered, then she shouted, "It's OK! Greer, I'm O —"

The double door on the far side of the room crashed open, and a high-intensity flashlight swept over the room.

Greer's drill sergeant voice barked out, "FBI! Hands where I can see them! Put your—"

But no one was listening. Greer froze, his eyes going wide like a frog on the highway catching an 18-wheeler's high-beams.

People were screaming, dragging their robes over themselves. One brave man dashed past Greer, disappearing into the night wearing nothing but a tiger mask.

Behind Sophie, she heard the young clerk also beating a hasty retreat.

The only person who was not running was the wide, sweating figure of Hunter Barnes, slipping his mask off his head as he stared at Greer in disbelief.

"Wh-what is the meaning of this!" the bookshop owner called out, swaying a touch unsteadily as he did.

Sophie, deciding to make the best of the situation, grabbed up the big man's robe and put it over his shoulders. "Hunter Barnes. FBI. We have a few questions, if you—actually, can you close your robe first?"

Chapter 21

Garden Books, and its owner Hunter Barnes, were a bust.

As she sat on the sidewalk, staring up at the rising moon, Sophie shook out her auburn hair, stretching her neck as she fought a yawn. It was a solid enough lead, and she couldn't just ignore the possibility that what was happening in that back room was connected to the murders. But Sophie still winced when she thought back over the signs that she'd misinterpreted.

His language had been flowery and poetic, but Barnes made it clear he was the ring leader of this psychedelic orgy group. Even in his questionably lucid state, he'd been able to provide an alibi for the murder of Maya Rossi, and when their backup arrived, Greer and Sophie had handed him over. The locals would want to follow up on the drugs and whatever indecency laws they chose to pursue.

The last thing Sophie had checked was the Tragedy mask she had seen hanging in the back room. It was a display piece, fused to its twin

Comedy mask without any straps. The eyeholes weren't even cutouts. They were painted black instead.

Coming up behind her, Greer clicked his tongue sympathetically and let out a soft grunt as he took a seat on the curb beside her.

"Well," he said. "That was... exciting."

Sophie couldn't help but let out a snort of laughter. "Yeah..." she croaked out softly. "But not nearly as fun as the last orgy I was at."

Greer's eyes shot wide and he rubbed at his neck awkwardly.

"I'm kidding," Sophie said, bumping him with her shoulder. "This one was *way* more fun."

Sophie noted the way her poor partner oscillated between confusion and embarrassment at the topic, his brain short-circuiting before her eyes.

"Wow, you are so gullible sometimes. I'm sorry, I'll stop now." Holding up a hand, Sophie let out a good-natured laugh, and Greer shook his head with a tired grin, letting out a quick sigh of relief.

Together they watched the Baton Rouge PD march Hunter Barnes to the back of a squad car, his robe precariously swaying as he tried to navigate the pavement on unsteady feet.

"Where do we go from here?" Sophie asked.

Greer checked his phone. The display showed it was nearly nine o'clock. If the killer kept up his pattern he could be at someone's home right now, perhaps drawing his knife this very moment. The thought sent a chill through Sophie, and she flexed her fingers in agitation. "There has to be something we can do," she said.

Greer folded his hands, resting his chin on his thumbs as he stared off in thought. "The books," he said at last. "Earlier you said they were the key."

"Our prime bookseller suspect turned out to be unconnected though," Sophie replied.

"True. But if the killer is being intentional, selecting these tragic manuscripts and pairing them to these particular people, maybe there's a pattern to them we're not seeing. I don't know about you, but I haven't read Shakespeare since high school."

Sophie considered the thought. "That's true. I played Juliet in the high school play, but I'm no expert," she noted off-handedly.

"No kidding," Greer said. "My high school did *Romeo & Juliet* too."

"Romeo?" Sophie asked.

Greer shook his head. "The priest."

"Somehow, that makes sense for you," she teased. They shared another look, likely each trying to picture the other strutting the boards of the high school auditorium, pubescent voices cracking as they stumbled through their lines. But the moment quickly passed and Sophie returned to her partner's idea. "I think you're right. We need an expert."

Greer was on his phone by the time she got the words out. "I know just the place," he said.

On his screen was a contact page for the Louisiana University of Arts and Sciences.

"LUAS?" she asked.

Greer nodded, bringing the phone to his ear. "The FBI has a good relationship with them. And we've pulled experts from their departments to help on other cases. They keep a late shift in the main office because of their international and night-course classes. Hello?" Swiveling his head slightly away, Sophie heard a faint greeting through the speaker on Greer's phone.

She pulled out her own cell phone, quickly searching up the university as Greer gave the woman on the line his FBI credentials.

"We were hoping to reach a Classics professor to consult on an ongoing case," he said politely. "...No, I'm afraid this is a matter of some urgency... Well, if you could simply pass on their contact information, we can reach out ourselves."

Suddenly the mild frustration building in Greer's face turned to grim focus. He lowered the phone and touched a button to put the receptionist on speaker. "Say that again, please."

The receptionist's digitized phone-voice sighed and with a huff, she said, "I mean to say that I'm not sure we can help you. Currently, we don't have a Classics or historical literature professor. Our last one was Professor Murphy, and he was let go about a month ago. We have his last known number, but he's not been responsive to our messages, and we haven't been able to reach him since."

Sophie met Greer's eyes, both of them feeling the same unease at the statement. She began to swiftly scroll and click through her own phone, chasing the new theory forming in her mind.

"I'm sorry to hear that," Greer said. "Can you tell me why Professor Murphy was let go?"

"I'm not sure I should say," the secretary replied hesitantly. "It's a somewhat delicate matter."

Greer kept his voice firm but sympathetic as he said. "We're not looking for an excuse to smear the school. And if you're worried, I can promise you your name won't be coming up in any report or conversation. But this is a murder investigation, and every detail may matter."

The secretary stifled a gasp, then asked cautiously, "You think Professor Murphy may have killed somebody?" Sophie's ear perked at this. Without seeing her body language, it was difficult to tell, but the vocal inflection hinted that, as frightening as the idea was... a part of the woman could already believe it.

"I'm not saying that," Greer replied diplomatically. "But as I said, we need to speak with an expert in classic literature. So why was Professor Murphy let go?"

The secretary paused, and Sophie could almost imagine her looking around the room before she spoke again in a low, office-gossip whisper. "He was going nuts. I mean, really erratic; unpredictable. We had a string of complaints from the girls, the female students in his department, saying he was asking them really uncomfortable questions about their relationships. Apparently, he threw a book at a young man's head because he said in class 'he wouldn't die for his girlfriend'. Then he went off on a huge tear when the department heads tried to confront him about his behavior, really insulting stuff, but mainly calling them small and insignificant. Saying they'd all be forgotten."

Sophie's stomach clenched. She froze, staring at her phone screen.

Greer shot Sophie a grave look as the secretary continued to list the gossip she had on Professor Murphy. and Sophie turned her cell phone to face him.

On the university website was a picture captioned *Professor Jordan Murphy, Classics*. It was a clean-shaven, middle-aged man in a black turtleneck leaning on a tall, wooden stool. He gave the photographer an impish, smirking stare.

Half of his face was concealed, covered by a weeping Tragedy mask held loosely in one hand.

Chapter 22

"You know, musicians are often destined for tragedy." The Mask gave a flick of his wrist, turning it in the air as if he were conducting an invisible orchestra, adjusting the volume of the Mozart filling the room to better enjoy the robust swell of the strings. "You're a sensitive breed. It's no small wonder so many of you meet your end to drugs or alcohol. I bet if I left you alone, you'd find your own tragic fate... but she wouldn't."

The Mask couldn't help but look again at the beautiful young woman set as the wallpaper image on his victim's cellphone.

"I should make a point of finding more people like you. If for no other reason than the quality of your home speakers," he said with a charmed laugh. "That and the depth and authenticity of your passion. You truly love your muse, don't you? You would go to hell and back for her."

The young man had a smoldering look in his one visible eye, the other was concealed by the shoulder-length hair falling over one side of his face. He was fighting the effects of the drugs in his bloodstream, huffing and groaning as his fingers coiled around the arms of his chair.

"Yes," he continued as if his restrained guest had been able to reply through the gag in his mouth. "I do believe you would do anything for her. And for your dear mother as well... but I'm getting ahead of myself."

The Mask settled a steaming bowl of broccoli florets, meeting his victim's eye line as he did. "Do try and hold off at least a few years before you kill yourself. Watching a gifted artist descend into madness is such a treat. It would be immoral to rob the world of your delicious downfall."

The young man glared, and behind his mask, the killer frowned. "Oh yes, they love a downfall," he said caustically.

The rose petals.

With sudden vim, he set to spreading the delicate flowers over the condo's main hallway, making his way to the front door.

A shadow crossed the frosted glass in the doorframe.

Already? The Mask shut off the lights, throwing himself against the wall beside a coat rack. Had she seen? He thought he'd have more time. He still needed to table the pork cutlets, and if he didn't pull the fuses, she'd simply turn on the lights and spoil the scene.

But his thoughts were interrupted by a sudden pounding on the door.

"Jacque! Open up." A man's voice, loud and insistent. Another harsh knock. "Man, I saw your lights on, I know you're in there. Just let me in."

The Mask ground his teeth, his jaw shifting in frustration as he watched the shadow on the other side of the door reach up to slam his fist against the wood once more. This wasn't right. This could ruin everything.

"I'm not leaving, man. We need to talk, so just—come on!"

The door rattled on its hinges as the man on the other side gave it a kick.

The Mask ran to the kitchen. Everything was in chaos now. The oven was beeping. He needed to pull the pork before it dried out, the wine needed time to breathe, and he hadn't even considered where to set the book.

Every detail mattered, every detail except for this-this brute! This classless moron kicking in the door.

He grabbed the kitchen knife. But as he did, the Mask's hand trembled... He looked at the musician tied up beside the dining table. The way he shook and tried to scream through his gag. The way the sound died in the clotted fabric. He looked at the large knife in his hand again.

No, that was for *her*. He couldn't reuse the same knife between a simple oaf and this prince's beautiful muse.

The Mask returned the knife to its block and began to throw open the kitchen drawers.

The man at the door shouted inarticulately, a new round of pounding knocks driving into the Mask's brain like a nail gun. At the dining room table, the musician's phone began to ring, a symphonic guitar riff under the digitized voice of a rock star jumping directly to the chorus of a song the Mask did not recognize. His heart was racing now, and he swore under his breath. It was too much. Too chaotic. This wasn't how any of this was supposed to happen.

There. A hammer.

Holding the heavy iron in one hand, the Mask rounded the kitchen doorway.

And with quick, determined strides, he made for the front door.

The shadow was gone.

Leaning close to the frosted glass, finding a bit of clear pane to see through, he caught sight of a man in a tank top walking backwards, away from the condo, rocking back on his heels and throwing two middle fingers toward the door every few steps.

For a moment, the Mask considered racing out after him. Tackling him and beating his skull in with the hammer anyway. His gloved hand squeezed the tool's rubber grip. No. That wasn't the story he would tell tonight.

Tonight was about love.

He let the hammer fall to the floor, dropping from his fingers as he returned to the musician.

"You need to consider your friends more carefully," the Mask said disapprovingly as he settled the aromatic pork and mushrooms onto a serving tray. "Rash fellows like that will only bring you to ruin. 'They stumble that run fast,' as the Bard once wrote."

He adjusted the feast on the table, lighting a few more candles. As he did, he saw the musician's cell phone once again. A missed call was noted on the screen. And a text message.

With a few quick taps, the Mask turned to his captive, smiling behind the weeping porcelain.

"It appears the fair muse is running late from work. We have time still." He pulled the book from an inner pocket, rolling the pages and turning it in his hands like a jeweler inspecting a stone. He had taken special pains with this one and bound the pages within their new cover himself. "Yes, we still have time to do things rightly. Perhaps an hour, she seems to think. Then the story begins."

Chapter 23

"Jordan Murphy, open up!" Greer pounded the door of the modest suburban home loud enough to be heard from the basement to the attic.

Through the drapes, Sophie could see the dim glow of a few lights, but no movement apart from the flicker of what might be a television screen in a far room.

"FBI! Open up or we will force the door."

Greer stepped back, drawing his pistol as he looked to Sophie. She drew her own gun and stepped to the side, giving him a nod that she was ready.

Taking a quick step forward, Greer launched his heel into the hardwood barrier, squarely targeting the space just above the door handle. Sophie heard a crack of splintering wood and a riotous slam as the door swung free and collided with the inside wall. His gun raised, Greer swept forward and Sophie followed, turning on the lights as she did.

They stayed within sight of each other, moving quickly from room to room.

As Sophie had thought, the TV in the living room was on, a classic movies channel was showing *Ben-Hur*, and the quiet roar of a Roman crowd cheering on a chariot race underscored their footsteps along with the creek of the front door still swaying on its hinges.

"Clear," Greer called, moving to the kitchen next.

Sophie opened a door into the attached garage. "No car," she said over her shoulder. "I don't think he's here."

Nevertheless, the pair kept their guns drawn as they checked a bedroom with a neatly made poster bed. A few other rooms were illuminated by dim night lights plugged into the outlets, and Sophie wondered if the former professor was attempting to use the running TV and small lights to convince his neighbors he was home, some small chance at an alibi if the need ever arose.

Trying a closed door near the bedroom, Sophie gave the brass-colored knob a twist, but the handle stuck fast, rattling in her grip.

"Locked?" Greer asked, coming alongside.

She frowned and pulled the lockpicks from her suitcoat. "Yes. And you know the only reason a person would keep locked doors in their own home. It's—"

There was another calamitous crash, and Sophie flinched as Greer's brown, leather shoe slammed into the door.

"Secrets, right?" Greer said giving Sophie a quick look as she returned the picks to her pocket. She shook her head, barely bothering to suppress the amused smile pulling at her lips.

She slipped past Greer, turning on the lights as she led the way.

Greer had driven the door open so forcefully that it now hung on one hinge, the other desperately clinging to the frame by the tenuous fingertip of a single screw. The room beyond was choked with bookshelves and smelled like candlewax and soot. A desk and chair with a cup of writing implements took up one complete wall, and where a window might be expected, instead, a corkboard was installed. It was littered with photographs. Amateurish and candid, many with dark outlines of blinds or leaves from trees and bushes to show they were taken from concealed positions.

Women. Men.

Couples on walks. Eating dinner. Laughing. Holding each other.

Dozens of them.

"Look."

Greer turned the front page of a scrapbook on the writing desk. Inside were more photographs. Sophie immediately recognized Josephine Ramsey and Jonny Sharpe. First by the picture of the pair making dinner together, apparently taken from their own back porch, then by the candlelit picture of Josephine's dead body.

Sophie felt her blood run cold. "He took this after he cut her throat. It's still dark. The candles are lit."

"He's drawn on the pictures," Greer said.

In a photo of Jonny Sharpe, a thin, silver marker had been used to overlay his ordinary business attire, drawing him in a toga with a laurel leaf around his scalp. "Marc Antony..." Sophie murmured, recalling the book left at Josephine's crime scene. "And Cleopatra," she finished, looking at the hieroglyphs drawn down the side of Josephine's picture.

Nodding with the grave seriousness of an undertaker, Greer tapped the next set of pictures. "Maya Rossi and her husband." More marker drawings obscured the photographs, and turning the next page, they found Marcus Baker and Eden Garza, the same collage of living, candid pictures and memorial shots of the recently murdered victims; the same silver marker dressing Eden in an Elizabethan gown.

Sophie looked away, anger and disgust making her fidget. The killer didn't care who they were, didn't care about the reality of their lives. He only cared how they fit his vision of the world, the stories he craved.

She stepped to the side, leaving Greer to close the scrapbook. The back of the desk was piled with books. A stack of photographs lay pushed against the books, but out of the pile, two pictures were pulled forward, as if Jordan Murphy had been considering them carefully from his seat.

Sophie leaned down to get a closer look.

The first picture was of a man and a woman at a café. The man was drawn with a sword at his hip, and a jeweled crown was added to the woman's head.

In the second picture, a man and woman were dancing together, flowers were drawn around them, and a wide cave mouth was added to the backdrop of the dance floor.

"It's one of these two," Sophie said. "He's preparing. Choosing. He's drawn on them the way he has the others in the book."

Sophie looked at the pictures, then at the stack of books. Frantically, she started sorting through them, glancing at titles, flipping a few loose pages. "There's a connection here. If we can just figure out what story he's referenced, maybe he's left a note or a hint about who they are."

A sword. A crown.

Flowers… caves…

Behind her, Greer was on his phone, calling for backup and to put out an APB on Jordan Murphy. "I'm sending you some photos. Unknown targets. We need facial recognition and any sort of ID program you can run on them as quickly as you can."

As he hung up, Greer grimaced at his phone. "Nine-fifty. Miss Quinn, if you have any miracles you're holding onto, now's the time."

"I know. I'm a hypnotist, not a wizard."

A wizard.

Sophie froze, glancing back at the pictures on the table.

A sword. A crown.

Hunting for just a moment, Sophie snatched a book from the pile, rapidly flipping the pages. As she did, a folded note, like a bookmark, fell out on the table.

"Judy Musea. Antonio Moore," Greer read. "There's an address here too."

Sophie slapped a palm on the photograph of the man and woman at the café. "That's them. I bet you anything that's the man's address."

Greer's jaw dropped as he stared from Sophie to the discovered note in disbelief. "How did you—?"

"*Le Morte d'Arthur*. It's the story of King Arthur. In it, his wife Queen Guinevere has an affair with his knight Sir Lancelot. It's another tragic romance story, just like the others. I thought of it when you said miracles. Merlin the wizard is a part of the story too, and—" waving her hands, Sophie waved away the thought like smoke, "It doesn't matter. The point is. That's one of the targets, and that's the address."

"Alright, let's go," Greer turned to the door, stopping with his hand on the frame when he saw Sophie was not following him.

"That's still only one possibility," she said. gesturing to the remaining picture. "What if they're the actual target? I have to figure this out."

"Then I'll stay with you, I'll get our backup to route to this address." Greer picked up his phone.

"Don't be ridiculous. It'll take them too long to organize and get someone there. Go. I'll be fine." With a wave, Sophie turned her back and sat at the desk, quickly paging through the next book in the stack.

Behind her, she could hear Greer starting to protest, but he knew she was right. They might already be out of time, and every second counted. And as his heavy footfalls retreated to the broken front door. Sophie was left alone.

Flowers. And a cave mouth.

Sophie flipped through the titles stacked on the desk. Minutes ticked by. There had to be something here. Something she was missing.

Opening the drawers, she found loose paper and what looked like bookbinding supplies. Thread and glue. Rolled leather and cardboard for covers. Yet another mystery on top of the questions she already had.

She picked up the picture again, looking at it closely. And her fingertip felt something, a change in texture? She rubbed her finger on the back of the photo, then turned it over. On the back was drawn a harp and a symbol like the circle and cross for 'female', but different: the top circle was detached, resting in a sort of cupping line at the top.

Closing her eyes, Sophie racked her brain for symbology texts, booklets, websites, any place she may have seen this image. And then it hit her. It was a medieval symbol. A sigil used in alchemy. It stood for Pluto.

Her mind was firing, bridging connections faster than she could articulate them. Pluto, a planet named for the Roman god of the underworld. She glanced to the cave mouth drawn on the front of the picture. "Pluto is the Roman name... in Greek he's Hades."

She dropped the photograph, returning to the book pile. There. A heavy volume compared to the rest. A collection that covered many ancient Greek myths, Ovid's *Metamorphoses*.

She flipped through the collection of translated poems.

A section was removed, several pages cut out with a razor from the look of the smooth edges. In their place was a folded note.

Two names. An address that was no more than a block away from her.

But the story was gone.

Of course, Sophie thought. It's not here because he leaves the books with his victims. But this was one part of a collection. Sophie looked back at the drawer of bookbinding supplies, then back to the fallen note with the address.

"He's there," she said, breathless and certain.

And she ran.

Chapter 24

From outside the condominium, Sophie could see the candlelight quavering in the darkened windows. She was sweating in the summer night air, out of breath from her sprint up the road from Jordan Murphy's home, but she held her pistol steady as she moved to the front door.

The windows around it were frosted. She couldn't see anything inside beyond the vague impression of firelight. With her ear to the door, though, she could hear the faintest hint of violin, orchestral music gently setting the mood the killer craved.

Backup on the way.

Sophie glanced to the door then back at the message Greer sent her a few seconds before.

Can't stay back. She typed back. *No time.*

For all she knew, the girl from the photograph, Ruby Fischer she had learned from the killer's note, was already dead. But if she wasn't, she soon would be. That is, if Sophie didn't act. She could imagine Greer, concern cutting a line through his forehead. But she couldn't play it safe just because—

Her phone buzzed with a fresh text.

Didn't say stay back. Save her. Backup on the way.

Then a second later, *B careful.*

Sophie smirked. Maybe this partnership would work out after all.

For a moment, Sophie considered the door. She might be able to break it by smashing the glass, but anything that disrupted the killer could put the victims' lives in danger. No, if she could sneak in, that would be much better. She took a step back.

Picking the lock would work, but it might take time. There was a keyhole in the handle as well as a deadbolt above it. Giving the handle a test pull, soft and quiet so as to not draw attention, Sophie felt both locks engage.

She stepped back, looking around at the windows. Maybe a back porch? Then Sophie saw it, just a tail of red fluttering through a window. A slender edge of a curtain at a bedroom window.

"Thank you, summer nights," Sophie whispered, running to the window.

It was on the first floor, the sill at chest height, but it was only open about eight inches or so. Beyond looked to be a man's bedroom, electric guitars and an overflowing hamper taking up most of the floor space while the unmade sheets trailed onto the floor. It was only lit by the moon and the adjacent streetlamp.

He must have already cut the fuses, Sophie thought.

No one was in the room, and the door to the main home was closed.

Working as quickly as she dared, Sophie tried to force the window open wider, but it wouldn't budge.

"Ok, that's fine," Sophie murmured. "Remember when you used to do straight-jacket escapes and water tanks and trick coffins? We can get in there. No problem. No—uff! Problem."

With one arm through, her shoulder and chest caught in the awkward opening. Sophie let out a huff, her eyes narrowing as she removed her jacket. She rolled it up and slipped the slate grey suit coat through the opening, letting it fall with a soft *tump* to the bedroom floor. "There. Now you *have* to get through."

She rolled her shoulders, rocking her neck back and forth as she took deep breaths in and out. She wasn't eighteen anymore, but at thirty-one, she had kept a fit figure and managed to avoid most of the pitfalls of life on the road. Being a traveling magician, one had to know their limits for fast food and how to squeeze in exercise wherever it fit. She had a bit more muscle too, built up from kickboxing and the martial training she went through preparing for the FBI entrance exams that she would never be allowed to take.

Yes, raw physique mattered, but the essential element of escape acts boiled down to fitting into spaces the audience believes you shouldn't fit through. And *that* came down to flexibility and breath control.

Sophie reached through the window with one hand, pulling herself up onto her toes. She tilted her head, raising her chin so she wouldn't tear her ears as she pushed herself through. It was tight. But if her head fit, she could make the rest of her fit. The head was the only part that wouldn't compromise with a bit of shimmying and angle work. And so, suppressing a hiss of pain as the hard plastic of the window slipped over her temples, past her jaw, and finally, behind her ears, Sophie let out a heavy breath of relief.

There ya go, kid. See. The benefits of not letting yourself get a big head, ha! Ron Gavriel's grandfatherly words echoed out of Sophie's memory as she hung in the window, one arm holding her up as she worked her legs up the siding, trying to find purchase to angle her other shoulder through.

Next came the other arm. Good.

Now her chest. Sophie reminded herself to get a new sports bra when this was over, wincing as she wormed her way forward, inhaling and exhaling to extremes as she manipulated her torso to a shape and size that would fit with every inch.

Come on! Shimmy those hips! Ron's specter called out.

Sophie worked her waist realizing that the last time she'd had to do this, her backside had been slightly more accommodating.

She could hear sounds in the home now. The classical music was swelling and a man's voice was sonorously declaiming something she couldn't quite make out. It had the cadence of ritual, like a pastor working his congregation up to the bits about 'fire and brimstone'.

He's nearly to the climax of his story, Sophie thought, grunting as she lifted a knee, adjusting her pants so she wouldn't lose them coming through the window.

You'll be behind a curtain, Ron's memory chastised, *so don't worry about looking ridiculous. Just get through before the drum roll!*

Sophie clenched her jaw, biting down against a groan as she pushed against the sill.

With a final turn of her hip, her waist came through.

Sophie barely caught herself, her hands landing on the soft cloth of her jacket on the floor. She turned herself around, rolling onto her elbows as she reoriented to a crouched position and put her jacket back on.

Pistol in one hand, she opened the bedroom door. Softly, by inches.

Now she could hear the man in the other room, she could see the candlelight's glow on the hallway walls in front of her.

"This is happening," the killer said. "Let it happen. Feel the pain, embrace the doom that's upon you. Let it happen, or it will get worse."

Jordan Murphy's voice did have a professorial quality to it. Clear and articulate, enunciating each word like it was poetry. Not strictly an accent, Sophie could forgive Marcus's first impression being that the man was 'British'.

She could hear a soft sound, like whimpering, only weaker, a sort of mewling. Sophie tested each step with her toe, trying to avoid creaks in the floorboards. She was closer now, passing by the front door; just around this corner would be the dining room.

Licking her lips, Sophie took a steadying breath and eased herself around the corner.

A dining table, the overwhelming scent of cooked pork and vegetables. Spices and sauces. Wine glasses sparkled in the candlelight as a man and a woman sat opposite each other, both sitting stiffly, tied to their chairs, swaying gently with the drugs Sophie knew were muddling their minds. Both with shoulder-length hair, the man in a sleeveless shirt, the woman in a flowing, floral top of brilliant tie-dye colors.

Behind the woman stood another man, caressing her hair with one hand, the other holding a broad kitchen knife beside her ear. He was covered head to foot in dark clothing, a black turtleneck and a white strap for a mask, stood out against his dark hair.

"Tonight, the meaningless mundanity of your bliss, will ascend to the immortal heights of true human experience. Misery. Tragedy. You must see this. She will die, but in the brutal strength of your surrender to it, you will spare another's life."

"Don't... touch her..." the man grunted, his eyes desperately trying to focus, to glare at the murderer holding his love hostage.

Sophie lifted her pistol, sighting the center of the masked figure's back.

At that moment, the young man's head swayed. He blinked as his eyes locked onto Sophie.

In the span of a heartbeat, the killer swung around, pivoting to put the young woman in the chair between him and Sophie.

She raced forward, shouting, "FBI! Drop the knife."

But he didn't. Instead, he pressed the knife to Ruby Fischer's throat, his weeping mask, the emblem of Greek Tragedy, met Sophie's own furious stare. "Step away," he commanded. "Drop the gun or I'll cut her neck now."

Sophie froze. She had the barest fraction of a second to decide if the killer was bluffing. Ritual was important to serial killers. Would he throw away his dramatic moment, just to show her he was serious? If he felt cornered or helpless, he might... he might...

"No, you won't," Sophie said, her voice more confident than she was, hoping to God she was making the right call.

The masked man pressed the knife closer, adjusting his grip as he pulled the girl's hair and drew a sedated whimper from her lips. "No?" he pressed. "I've done it before. Or did you come here still thinking the boyfriend over there would be the killer?"

He's already bragging, Sophie thought. Despite his aggression, he's talking... looking for... validation? Awe?

Sophie took a half-step closer, masking it as simply adjusting her footing. "I've seen your work. Aeneas and Dido. Antony and Cleopatra. Romeo and Juliet feels a bit mainstream, but I imagine by now you're hitting the edge of your knowledge, Professor Murphy."

The masked figure seemed taken aback, going rigid, the knife twitching as he unconsciously adjusted his grip.

Taking advantage of his stunned silence, Sophie edged another step closer. "Yes, I know about your dismissal from the university. That's what this is really about, isn't it?"

"You have no idea what you're talking about!" the killer shouted. "This is about life. It's about meaning and truth and the beauty of despair. It's not about an office in a second-rate—"

"But it is." Sophie snapped.

It was a gamble, arguing with him like this. But backup would be coming. She just had to keep him busy. And the more she saw him, his hunched posture, hiding from the gun behind a girl and a knife, the more she was starting to see the shape of his mind. He was in control when he had time to prepare, to plan. But now, things were off-script. He'd be impressionable, suggestible. He was looking around, trying to figure out an escape, what to do now that he was cornered.

"Hey!" Sophie shook her pistol as she shouted out. "Pay attention when I'm talking." If she kept him reactive, paralyzed, trying to analyze his current problem, she could buy more time. "You think you're being clever. Laying out references and books you think most people won't figure out. Maybe you're even trying to paint yourself as the tragic hero of this story, burdened with knowledge about the true, cruel face of the world. Boo-hoo."

One half-step at a time, Sophie sidled around the table, Murphy moving opposite her and keeping the girl between them until he bumped his hip against the dinner table, sending the plates rattling and the candle shivering in the dark condo.

"Stop that! Stop trying to get around me!" he shrieked.

She was only three feet from him now, Ruby Fischer and her tie-dye blouse were pulled away from the table, her chair squeaking as Murphy tried to keep his human shield between him and the gun.

"You're not in a Tragedy," Sophie sneered. "You're a clown. A self-righteous buffoon in a Comedy, too self-absorbed to see how insane your own actions are."

With a scream, half panic and half rage, Murphy shoved his hostage forward. Sophie threw one hand forward to catch her as the chair overturned. With her other hand, she fired the pistol.

The shot whistled past Murphy, burying itself in the rear wall of the condo as he swung his knife wildly for Sophie's arm. With a scream of pain, Sophie pulled back her pistol hand, a fresh line of red blood spreading on her suit sleeve. Before she could adjust, though, the blade came back, and Sophie fell to the floor, Ruby Fischer tumbling beside her as she dove out of the way. She tried to realign her pistol with her injured arm, the white face of Murphy's weeping mask, coming for her like a ghost from the darkness.

She squeezed the trigger just as his black-booted foot connected with her wrist, her second shot driving a hole through the ceiling as the gun spun from her hand.

Then he was on her. Grabbing his knife hand by the wrist, Sophie drove the heel of her palm up into the mask, once, twice.

The hard material cracked, then chipped away as Murphy tumbled off of her, rolling to his side.

When he looked up again, the mask hung limply, one crazed eye, rimmed with blood from a cut on his nose, was staring through the broken gap while the other was still hidden by the damaged ceramic.

He charged Sophie again, scurrying forward on hands and knees like a rat, the knife raised, the blade pointed down like a fang as he tried to drive it into Sophie's neck.

Throwing out a kick, Sophie connected with his upraised forearm and drove Murphy's knife hand against the side of his head. She kicked him again, this time aiming directly for his head. The killer wobbled in place, the knife falling from nerveless fingers as he slumped onto all fours. With a final roaring shout, Sophie shot her heel forward one last time, driving the broken face of the mask into Jordan Murphy's nose.

The killer dropped, his limbs sprawling as his head thudded against the hardwood floor.

Sophie took a deep breath, wincing as she put pressure on her slashed arm to move to a crouch. First, she stared at Murphy, giving him a second or two to recover from unconsciousness to see if she might need to kick him again. Next, she found her gun. Once both these things were done, Sophie grabbed the knife Murphy had dropped and cut Ruby Fischer free. She was in no way articulate, her eyes unfocused and drifting while she tried to sit up.

"Easy, easy," Sophie said, helping her to a seated position by the wall. "Help is on the way. I'm going to get your boyfriend untied now, ok?"

Rubbing her eyes, Ruby moved her chin in a way that might have been a yes. Regardless, Sophie moved to the end of the dining table, sawing away at the young man's bindings. She was through the cords at his feet when she heard a thudding commotion across the room. A muffled squeal of fear.

Sophie shot to her feet, drawing her pistol once more.

Murphy was standing again. His mask was gone now, his broken nose mashed and crooked as blood ran down over his split lips. One eyebrow was cut and swollen, the other eye wide and bloodshot. With one arm, he held his victim, dragging her with a hand around her throat as he moved past the front door.

"Stop! Stay where you are!" Sophie called, quickly rushing to follow.

As she did, she saw that Murphy's other hand now held a hammer. Where did he get that?

"I said, freeze!" Sophie called again.

But if he heard her, Murphy didn't respond. Instead, he only smiled over his victim's shoulder as he opened a door behind him.

A basement.

Sophie saw the glitter of a glass bulb above the steps. But with the fuses pulled, just like the rest of the home, it was dark.

On the first step, shadow wrapped the pair, casting Murphy's face in a jack o' lantern grin. And within two steps, they vanished entirely.

Chapter 25

Backup is coming.

I should just stay here. He's trapped down there, and once we have more people, we can... we will... Sophie let out a desperate sigh. Once we have more people, he won't think he can win anymore. He'll bash in Ruby Fischer's skull with a hammer and then let himself be caught or gunned down.

Sophie wiped at the sweat beading on her forehead, anxious at the thought of the young woman being held hostage down below. In her mind's eye, she pictured Ruby Fischer, long dark hair over her tie-dyed blouse, a serial killer's arm around her throat as he lifted the hammer in the other hand. Then Ruby's face became Molly's face. There had been a moment, that night when Molly had died and Sophie had lived, when Sophie could have escaped. She'd opened the lock around her ankle. She was under the boat. She could have swum away. But her sister was still up there.

Sophie stared into the abyss of the pitch-dark basement in front of her. Her fingers coiled around her gun's grip as she felt her chest rise and fall with a nervous breath. She hadn't been able to save Molly. But that didn't mean it was the wrong choice. Here and now, she had the same choice. And there was no other conclusion. Backup wasn't a saving grace, it was a time limit, a countdown to the final victim's death. Sophie opened her phone, switching on the flashlight.

With slow careful steps, she descended into the basement.

Compared to the summer air above, the basement was cool, and Sophie could see the glisten of condensation on the concrete walls as her phone's light cast around. When the stairwell opened up, she saw that the cellar's footprint was much larger than she expected. Apart from a few concrete support columns, it looked like hundreds of square feet, perhaps ten yards to a side, but it was choked with rows of shelving. In the first few moments, she found deflated basketballs, baseball mitts, plastic tubs with duct tape labels like 'Christmas' and 'Winter Clothes', and an Elvis Presley cookie jar. Even the floor between was hazardous with loose bike wheels and fallen shovels, garden hoes, and paint cans stuck wherever a shelf or wall hook couldn't be found to hold them.

Between the rows, at the edge of Sophie's light, something moved. She quickly adjusted her aim, shadows flaring and warping. Every coat tree and discarded lampshade became the outline of Jordan Muphy, his broken nose and crazed eyes glimmering out of every coil of Christmas lights and tupperware bin of spare batteries.

"I expected brave Orpheus to be the one to come down here. Her lover, descending to hell for his love. But you... You are obsessive aren't you?" Murphy's voice was garbled, the swelling in his smashed face was muddling his words, but his natural articulation carried him through. He spoke carefully as if from a stage. But while Sophie listened, she found she could not follow the source of the voice. The metal and concrete of the basement, along with the claustrophobic rows of detritus, were casting strange echoes. And as she walked between the shelves, she couldn't tell if the pops and clicks around her were Murphy creeping in the darkness or a startled rat simply trying to evade her l ight.

"It doesn't matter," Murphy continued. "We are all in the underworld, regardless of the roles we play. Tonight, I am Hades, holding sweet Eurydice by the throat. Tomorrow, you may be the god of death, and I your helpless captive. Will you play me a song to win her back, gentle Orpheus?" The maniac cackled, his voice descending into a gagging cough as he spat what sounded like a glob of phlegm or blood onto the fl oor.

"Let her go, Murphy," Sophie said, scanning the spaces between the rows. "If you give up now, you can get out of this alive."

A series of tutting clicks rolled out of the dark. "That's not how Tragedies work, my dear," Murphy said in a sing-song voice.

It was troubling that she couldn't hear Ruby at all. Perhaps the sedatives had taken full effect and she was unconscious now, or perhaps in the minute Sophie had taken at the top of the stairs, the madman had broken her neck. Sophie tried not to think about stumbling on the poor young woman's body in the dark. No. He wouldn't kill his last bargaining chip. He would use her to escape. As long as he still believes he can.

Sophie bit her lip and tried not to think of the imminent backup and what Murphy may do when he is well and truly trapped.

A screaming cry erupted from the darkness behind her, and Sophie spun just in time to duck Murphy's hammer, instead, taking a knee to the stomach as the killer rammed into her. Metal clanged on metal as he struck the shelves and Sophie's muzzle flare lit up the room like a lightning flash. The deafening gunshot from her reactive fire drove out all other sound, and Sophie could only hear ringing for the few seconds she wrestled with Murphy, their tangled bodies knocking the shelves behind her over, glass and plastic silently shattering and bounding all around as the falling shelf dominoed into the next.

Murphy's hammer came down on the concrete beside Sophie's head, and he dove away as she turned her gun on him. Like a spider, he crawled under the nearest shelf, and as the ringing in Sophie's ears began to subside, she heard the flapping of his boots on the concrete floor as he ran into the darkness.

Her heart pounding, Sophie looked around in wild fear. This was no good. With her phone light, he could see her all the time, but she could only see him when he attacked. No, this was going to get her killed. Grimacing, and hoping to God that Ruby Fischer wasn't buried under the collapsed shelving behind her, Sophie turned off her phone's flashlight.

The blackness was absolute. Carefully, Sophie crept along the row. One step at a time, feeling her way to not bumble into anything that would give away her location.

"Interesting," Murphy's choking voice mused. "Now you choose the darkness."

She could hear his boots, short, sporadic movements. He started and stopped like a game of red-light-green-light. Swallowing, trying to force the ringing in her ears to dissipate Sophie edged closer, listening, waiting.

A slam echoed from the top of the stairs. Another. And then the sound of breaking wood.

Sophie bit back a cry of warning.

"FBI!" shouted several voices as booted feet crashed across the floor above their heads.

"We have a survivor!" another voice called, no doubt at the sight of Ruby's boyfriend still sedated at the dining room table.

Sophie closed her eyes despite the darkness, trying to focus, trying to separate the small sounds of Murphy's movements against the louder sounds of the agents above storming the condo.

"Miss Quinn," a strong voice called out, commanding and coarse yet warm like a sun-baked stone. Greer called out again, "Miss Quinn, where are you?"

Oh, no. Sophie quickly buried her phone in her jacket. If she knew Greer, the next thing he would do is try to call her. Her phone would buzz and light up, then—

Sophie heard a small squeak of rubber and froze. Carefully, she turned her shoulders, not daring a noise from her shoes or the possibility of tripping. She peered into the dark, her eyes open as wide as she could manage. Gingerly, she lifted her pistol.

In a flash, the basement light behind her turned on with an electric hum, and Sophie started.

The fuses.

Beside her, raising a hammer over her head, stood Jordan Murphy. In the same moment the room burst into light, he screamed and his free hand came up, shielding his eyes as he swung the hammer down.

At the last moment, Sophie stepped aside, the hammer's grip coming down on her shoulder with a painful thud as she pulled the trigger.

Two pops. The gunfire deafened her once more.

Jordan Murphy blinked, his eyes acclimating to the light, focusing for one more breath before they went blank; the hammer and his head both hit the ground with a decisive crack.

Chapter 26

"Yep. No more sleeveless dresses for me," Sophie said with mock resignation.

Greer gave a small chuckle, looking down at the stitches across Sophie's forearm. "What do they usually do about that in showbusiness?"

Pursing her lips, Sophie sat back against the hospital's plastic bench and blew out a sigh. "Makeup. Sometimes a tattoo if you're the type of act that can pull it off. What do you think? Navy anchor? or hula girl?"

Greer only laughed again. It was a quiet, considerate laugh, which was fair. Neither had slept yet.

They'd been at the scene for hours while Sophie gave her statement and walked their backup through the crime scene. An EMT was able to patch up her arm once the drug-addled Ruby Fischer and her boyfriend were strapped into their ambulance, both confused and sedated but very much alive. Still, Greer had insisted on a follow-up at the hospital for Sophie's cut, raising several concerning points about blood-to-blood contact with a homicidal maniac.

In telling her partner she didn't need a ride away from the hospital, she'd let slip that she was sticking around because her father was having surgery that morning. Funny enough, after that bit of information, Greer decided he didn't much feel like sleeping yet.

Sophie told herself that she was just too tired to protest, but as they sat there together, waiting, she found the strong-armed agent's presence calming. Comforting. Minutes ticked by in silence, and Sophie found herself slipping further and further back, trying to find some comfortable level of slouch in the hard plastic.

Without saying a word, just having Greer here next to her was... nice. Yes. That was the word. Nice.

...

"Sophie!"

Waking with a start, Sophie blinked away the harsh hospital fluorescents, rubbing at her eyes. Flashbacks of her childhood came back as Sophie's mother called out her name again.

At least someone had given her a pillow, Sophie thought for one sleep-addled moment. Then in the space of a mortifying heartbeat, Sophie's brain tried to rationalize why a pillow might feel like a man's shoulder.

Her eyes went wide, and Sophie shot ramrod straight in her seat, nearly knocking Greer from the waiting room bench as she pushed off his arm.

Her flowing summer dress swishing around her knees, Zadie Quinn rushed to her daughter's side as a bald doctor with a walrus mustache hustled to keep up. "It's a miracle," she said, grabbing Sophie by the shoulders and giving her a little shake as she blinked back tears "A miracle! He's awake. *Cher*, your daddy's going to be a-ok."

It felt as though a gust of wind had shot through Sophie's whole body. She let out a breath and felt a little light-headed as she took her mama by the arms and pulled her into an embrace. "That's wonderful," she said, the words feeling completely inadequate to the sensation.

Her father was stable and awake. He was going to live.

As Sophie stood and helped her mother to her feet, the doctor cleared his throat. "Yes. He's stable and responding well to initial assessments, so you can all feel free to go in and see him whenever you're ready. We'll be checking in on him every fifteen minutes for the next few hours, and I'd like to keep him an extra day or two just to be safe—"

"We're getting out of here, Sophie!" her mother crowed as tears of joy spilled out of her eyes. "At last, we're going home."

As the words left her mouth, Zadie seemed to notice Greer's presence for the first time. She looked from Sophie to Greer, then back, her mouth scrunching up in a smile that she was completely failing to swallow, and Sophie could see the gears turning in her mother's head. "I know you," she said coyly. "So good to see you again, Mr. Greer."

"Mrs. Quinn," Jonathan Greer said, as charming and polite as ever. "I'm so glad to hear your husband is going to be alright. I understand it was quite a scare for a good while there."

"Thank you," she said earnestly. "And I appreciate you supporting and watching out for our little Sophie, here. I know she can be a real *handful.*"

Greer let out a good-natured laugh, resting his thumbs on his belt with a shrug. "Well, we had a rough start, but I think we make a great team now."

"Oh," Zadie said, tilting her head provocatively. "You two are a *team* then?"

"All right," Sophie quickly interjected. "Thank you, Mama. The doctor said we can see Daddy, so let's get. Okay?"

She didn't think of it until the words were out of her mouth, but in the moment, Sophie's accent, the careful East Coast flavor she'd cultivated for her performances, evaporated, and the Cajun of her childhood came back in full. As soon as she realized, she cleared her throat, her cheeks feeling hot as she shook her head. What was the matter with he r?

On cue, Zadie Quinn voiced her enthusiastic agreement, turning and following the doctor up the hallway. But as she did, Sophie lingered back.

“I’m sorry about her,” she said apologetically.

Greer held up a palm. “It’s alright, Miss Quinn. I know how mothers are. I have one myself.”

Sophie let out a soft laugh, then chewed her lip. She started to turn, stopping and swaying on her feet for a moment before turning back to Greer.

“I think we’re a little past ‘Miss Quinn’ at this point, don’t you?”

Greer met her eye, and Sophie shrugged, looking away before the blush in her cheeks grew even hotter. “Why don’t you just call me Sophie?”

With a gentle smile, Greer gave the smallest inclination of a nod. “Alright then. Sophie.”

Epilogue

Sophie pondered if she should have brought Greer in on this.

Specifically, as she caught the first fishing-line glimmer of a trip wire and wondered if it was the same type they'd encountered in their last investigation together, attached to a claymore mine, ready to blow away her legs or worse, she found herself reassessing her decision not to tell the former Marine engineer about her plan.

But ultimately, alone among the summer cicadas and the barking tree frogs, Sophie decided this was better. He'd done enough for her. He and Merchant both. Though, with the thought came a fresh wave of guilt.

Your battle is my battle. That's what he'd said to her.

But as she reached the militia compound's electric perimeter fence, Sophie resigned herself to the fact that, if nothing else, it was too late to go back now.

Sophie had failed to meet her contact within the Mississippi Line Minutemen. She wasn't there when he went to receive her payment, and when she tried to reach out to him again, the encrypted line he'd used was dead.

He was gone.

And that meant any leads into RK's identity, his past with the militia group, would have to be bought with Sophie's own skill and effort.

The electric fence in front of her hummed with the promise of excruciating pain to anyone dumb enough to try and climb it. Though, from the razor wire loops that crowned the barrier, climbing didn't seem like a winning idea to begin with.

Wrapped in black, under an equally dark ski mask, Sophie Quinn was invisible. Still, she examined the ground until she found a spot where two bushes bunched together, parting the foliage enough to shimmy under its leafy cover.

Then, she settled in to wait.

Fifteen minutes later, a patrol passed her. Two men, one smoking a cigarette and both holding powerful-looking rifles, strolled past. To any casual observer, they looked like they could have been plucked from any town between Mobile and Austin with their close-cut hair and the mix of dad-bod and muscle that some liked to call 'fit-fat' or as Sophie had heard more than once, 'what a *real man* looks like'. However, the impression only lasted until they were close enough for the compound's area lights to reveal the military fatigues and Kevlar tactical vests each man wore.

Sophie held her breath as they passed by. An hour later, the same pair passed, sans cigarette. Finally, after another hour, her skin beginning to itch from lying in the grass, Sophie watched them pass for a third time.

An hour. That's all the time the patrol took to reach this part of the fence. She would need to be in and out, and hopefully deep into the bayou, before that hour was up.

When the patrol had disappeared from sight, Sophie crept forward until she could reach out and touch the humming fence.

From the satchel at her waist, a dollar-store fanny pack she'd spray-painted midnight blue, she pulled out a spool of copper wire and a steel tent stake.

Tying off one end of the wire to the stake, she drove it into the ground. Then, clipping off the other end with a pair of wire cutters, she fashioned the loose end into a crook.

Holding her breath, Sophie tilted the crook forward and let it drop.

The wire hooked the fence with a few spitting sparks on impact. The humming seemed to intensify and Sophie thought for a moment it may set fire to even the damp grass around her. Instead, when the humming whine reached its crescendo, it abruptly stopped.

The sound was gone. Still holding her breath, Sophie gingerly tapped the fence with the back of her gloved hand.

Nothing.

Not even wasting a moment for a sigh of relief, Sophie took her wire cutters to the shorted-out fence, cutting a line only large enough for her to slip through on hands and knees.

The compound was what she imagined from the satellite images she'd found in Merchant's USB. Barracks. Armory. Private quarters for the few men who acted as officers in the off-grid group. And Sophie's destination.

The central office was a squat, square building with an attached radio tower rising ten meters into the air above it and a satellite dish.

In the dead of night, Sophie didn't imagine there would be many of the militiamen walking around, and she was glad to see this was the case. It was a ghost town between the spartan buildings at the heart of the compound.

And after a few minutes with her lockpicks, she was in.

A couple laptops and an ancient-looking desktop computer were hooked up on a broad desk against one wall along with radios of varying designs and strengths. Muted televisions tuned to news stations around the globe were running opposite this arrangement, and between them stood several clusters of filing cabinets.

Annoyingly, despite the low-tech security being used, the militiamen seemed diligent in locking up behind themselves, and Sophie found minutes slipping by as she picked the file drawers one by one.

A lot of it was simply receipts. Weapons. Equipment. When they bought it and where. Then there were the militia company records. Training exercises. Performance reviews. Officer recommendations. It was extremely and meticulously detailed in the way only people with genuine enthusiasm for their work can do.

Sophie checked her phone. She was nearly out of time. If the patrols found her hole in the fence, well, she wasn't sure what an alarm raised in the compound would look like, but it couldn't be pretty.

Taking a deep breath, Sophie closed her eyes.

It's old information. A decade or more back. Where does it make sense to keep that?

When she opened her eyes, Sophie snapped her gloved fingers and made a beeline around the file cabinets. She circled them, looking them up and down. Looking for any signs of wear or...

Rust.

This had to be it, the oldest looking cabinet, set in a corner of the group, a handle loose from its use over the years. Less than a minute later, stowing her picks back in her satchel, Sophie found what she was looking for.

Personnel files. Membership logs. All of it going back—

Sophie stopped, her vision swimming for a moment as her hands trembled.

It was a group photo. Nine people lined up in gear similar to the patrol she saw. Eight of them might have been faceless mannequins for all Sophie could see; her attention was fixed on the tall man second from the end.

A man in a baseball cap pulled low over his eyes. The sun's shade a mask over his features. But held between the fingers of his left hand was a cigar, and on one bare arm was a tattoo. Dark. Geometric. A design that made no physical sense, but one Sophie could trace in her mind perfectly.

It was him.

But as the shock began to subside, it was quickly replaced as Sophie took in the complete picture.

Nine people. But only eight men.

The River Killer wasn't just standing next to a comrade in arms, he had his cigar-bearing arm around the shoulder of a young woman also in militia fatigues, his capped head turned down as he bent in to kiss her smiling cheek.

A face Sophie had seen only a few nights before at a high-stakes poker table in Baton Rouge.

Miriam Carter-Blanc.

Mimicking the woman's words, RK's graveyard voice whispered in Sophie's mind, *Well well, I suppose that's jus' your bad luck, eh cher?*

What's Next for Sophie Quinn?

The Siren's Song – Book 4

"He's killing them for you, Sophie. All for you."

In the sweltering summer heat of the Louisiana delta, internationally famous stage-magician turned FBI consultant, Sophie Quinn, is closing in on the man who murdered her sister. The River Killer. But just when Sophie thinks she's ahead, a new player appears to make her wonder if all the progress in her investigation hasn't been part of someone else's game.

Messages and clues embedded in the crime scenes of a new string of killings make Sophie question her own sanity and wonder if the ghosts of her past are much, much closer than she'd feared.

As Sophie's world unravels, threatening to tear the people closest to her away forever, she must decide just how much blood she's willing to have on her hands for her revenge, and whether she can ever really come home again.

Also by Georgia Wagner

Once a rising star in the FBI, with the best case closure rate of any investigator, Ella Porter is now exiled to a small gold mining town bordering the wilderness of Alaska. The reason for her new assignment? She allowed a prolific serial killer to escape custody.

But what no one knows is that she did it on purpose.

The day she shows up in Nome, bags still unpacked, the wife of the richest gold miner in town goes missing. This is the second woman to vanish in as many days. And it's up to Ella to find out what happened.

Assigning Ella to Nome is no accident, either. Though she swore she'd never return, Ella grew up in the small, gold mining town, treated like royalty as a child due to her own family's wealth. But like all gold tycoons, the Porter family secrets are as dark as Ella's own.

Also by Georgia Wagner

The skeletons in her closet are twitching...

Genius chessmaster and FBI consultant Artemis Blythe swore she'd never return to the misty Cascade Mountains.

Her father—a notorious serial killer, responsible for the deaths of seven women—is now imprisoned, in no small part due to a clue she provided nearly fifteen years ago.

And now her father wants his vengeance.A new serial killer is hunting the wealthy and the elite in the town of Pinelake. Artemis' father claims he knows the identity of the killer, but he'll only tell daughter dearest. Against her will, she finds herself forced back to her old stomping grounds.

Once known as a child chess prodigy, now the locals only think of her as 'The Ghostkiller's' daughter.

In the face of a shamed family name and a brother involved with the Seattle mob, Artemis endeavours to use her tactical genius to solve the baffling case.

Hunting a murderer who strikes without a trace, if she fails, the next skeleton in her closet will be her own.

Want to know more?

Greenfield press is the brainchild of bestselling author Steve Higgs. He specializes in writing fast paced adventurous mystery and urban fantasy with a humorous lilt. Having made his money publishing his own work, Steve went looking for a few 'special' authors whose work he believed in.

Georgia Wagner was the first of those, but to find out more and to be the first to hear about new releases and what is coming next, you can join the Facebook group by copying the following link into your browser www.facebook.com/GreenfieldPress.

About the Author

Georgia Wagner worked as a ghost writer for many, many years before finally taking the plunge into self-publishing. Location and character are two big factors for Georgia, and getting those right allows the story to flow seamlessly onto the page. And flow it does, because Georgia is so prolific a new term is required to describe the rate at which nerve-tingling stories find their way into print.

When not found attached to a laptop, Georgia likes spending time in local arboretums, among the trees and ponds. An avid cultivator of orchids, begonias, and all things floral, Georgia also has a strong penchant for art, paintings, and sculptures.

Printed in Great Britain
by Amazon

30775315R10136